EVERGLADES ADVENTURE

EVERGLADES ADVENTURE

Stephen W. Meader

ILLUSTRATED BY CHARLES BECK

SOUTHERN SKIES

ISBN 978- 1-931177-66-5 cloth
ISBN 978-1-931177-67-2 paperback

Library of Congress Catalog Card Number 57-10350

SOUTHERN SKIES

LITTLE ROCK, ARKANSAS

www.southernskies.com

Dedication

The republication of this book is dedicated with love to the memory of Mary Theressa Atchley by her little brother, Jerry Atchley.

EVERGLADES ADVENTURE

Toby Morgan slammed the tattered old Latin book shut and leaned back, hands clasped behind his head. Outside the open window a constant twitter of small birds called him, and a soft, beguiling trade wind rustled the palmetto thatch.

What difference would two more pages of Caesar's *Gallic War* make, when all the delights of a Florida spring lured him to action? He knew the answer well enough. Back in September, when they had moved from New Jersey to their new home in Fort Dallas, he had made a solemn promise to his invalid father that he'd keep up with his schoolwork.

Dr. Morgan had been a general practitioner and a good one. When the war came in 1861, he had volunteered as an Army surgeon and served in the crowded field hospitals for four hard years. Then, coming home after Lee's surrender, he had continued to overwork as he tried to take care of all the sick people within miles. Finally, in 1870, his health had broken. His body was racked by rheumatism, and a constant, hollow cough betrayed a weakness in his lungs.

Knowing that he must have sun and rest to stay alive, he took what little money he had been able to save,

7

packed his family aboard a coastwise steamer, and started south.

Sixteen-year-old Toby would never forget that trip. The side-wheeler was none too seaworthy, and they ran into rough weather almost as soon as they passed Delaware Breakwater. Both the boy's parents were desperately seasick. His sister Betsy, who was ten, recovered after a day of it, and the two youngsters had the run of the decks, for most of the other passengers stayed in their cabins. Clinging to the rails of the pitching ship, Toby and Betsy rode out a gale off Cape Hatteras, wondering if the next great wave would swamp them. Then, on the fourth day, they came out into sunshine and the sparkling blue water of the Gulf Stream.

Passengers began to appear on deck. A few were decent people like themselves. Others were of a different stripe. They were the "carpetbaggers"—mean-faced, greedy men, hurrying to grab what pickings they could find in the prostrate South. The Morgans were glad to see most of them leave the vessel at Charleston or Savannah. Only two or three went on as far as St. Augustine, the last port of call before Key West. The doctor and his family had the steamer almost to themselves on the balmy run down the Florida coast.

When they reached the little town at the tip of the keys, it was a week before Dr. Morgan was able to charter a fishing schooner that would take them north again to Fort Dallas. Toby spent the time nosing around the harbor and hunting shells on the beach. The men he saw around the docks were an unsavory crowd—dirty and unshaven. They eyed him sullenly, wondering, he was sure, if he had enough money to make him worth robbing.

Key West in those days was a rough place. Some of the "conch" inhabitants owned fishing boats, but there were more who lived by beachcombing, smuggling, and pillaging the frequent wrecks that washed ashore. They were of mixed races—Cubans, Bahamians, and assorted Americans.

A day and a night in the smelly little schooner brought the Morgans and their possessions into Biscayne Bay. There was a ramshackle dock at the mouth of the Miami River, and there the trunks and odds and ends of furniture they had brought from the North were dumped without ceremony. The conch skipper took his pay and promptly sailed away, and there they were left, strangers in a strange land.

Toby had a vivid recollection of that day. The sky was bright overhead, and the coconut palms, back from the water, waved their fronds gracefully in the breeze. But the place appeared as deserted as Robinson Crusoe's island.

Finally, from a weather-beaten frame house behind the trees, a stout man in a wide straw hat came hobbling down to the dock. He introduced himself as Charles Peacock.

"Run a coontie mill up river," he explained, "an' keep a sort o' boardin' house. No boarders right now, though. You folks got any place to stay?"

Gratefully they accepted lodgings at the boarding house until they could buy or build a house. After some questioning Toby found out that "coontie" was a starchy flour ground from a native root. It was used for bread, made in the Indian style.

They saw only one other white person that day. She was Mrs. Egan, a rawboned, taciturn woman whose family had been early settlers in the region. She owned, they were glad to discover, an old, unused house back in the palmetto scrub. And she would rent it to them for five dollars a month, "long as ye want to stay."

For two back-breaking weeks Toby had hacked away at the brush, clearing a dooryard. The house itself was sturdy enough, though strange looking. It was built for the most part of old ships' timbers, and several of its small windows were former cabin portholes. The flooring was sound teak and mahogany.

Mr. Peacock showed the boy how to repair the thatched roof with palmetto fronds. By the end of October he had it fixed so well that hardly a drop came through, even in the heaviest showers.

From the start there had been Indians around. They were Seminoles, out of the Everglades, who came down to the tiny settlement to trade. A Mr. William Brickell had recently settled in Fort Dallas and opened a sort of store, where he sold such necessities as salt pork, molasses, tea and coffee. He also had a barrel of Cuban rum under the counter, and knives, beads, and bright-colored calico, which he traded for the otter, deer, and alligator skins brought in by the Indians.

The Seminoles had a campground on the farther side of the stream. There they would array themselves in all their finery—buckskin breeches, red shirts, strings of beads and shells—and paddle their dugouts across to the dock. The squaws and children were dressed in the same outlandish fashion.

They would squat on the sand in a row and gravely watch the comings and goings of the few white settlers.

At first it made Toby nervous to have a silent audience as he sweated in the scrub. After a few days he had become used to it and even drew one of the older Seminole men into a conversation of sorts. Part of it was in sign language, part in very broken English, and part in the Seminole tongue. Before he knew it, the boy had picked up a few Indian words and phrases.

The Seminoles made very little trouble except when

they got hold of liquor. This was what they always wanted in trade, and Mr. Brickell had to be careful how he doled out his rum. If a few of the braves got drunk, they whooped and hollered, danced and shot off guns at their camping place. The next day they lay like logs, snoring wherever they had happened to fall, while the squaws sat placidly fanning the flies away.

Until she became accustomed to having Indians about, Mrs. Morgan was afraid to stir outside. She fully expected to be scalped some dark night. It was a surprise to the whole family to find that these Seminoles were not only harmless but honest. They were curious about white people's belongings, but there was no stealing, even though houses were left unlocked.

Thirty years earlier there had been massacres and burnings along the South Florida coast. The long and bloody Seminole wars had finally petered out, leaving the remnants of the tribe unconquered. They seemed to bear no resentment toward the white men and were ready to live at peace as long as they were left alone in their Everglades hunting grounds.

By the time the Morgans moved into their house, Toby had begun to enjoy his new life. He still had plenty of work to do, for there was a garden to plant and they had acquired a cow, a pig, and a few chickens. But even with his daily chores and studies, he found time for exploring.

First of all there was the beach. He had patched up an old boat, lent him by Mr. Peacock, and rowed across Biscayne Bay to the outer key. Most of the low island was covered with mangrove jungle, but on the seaward side there was a fine stretch of coral sand. The breakers that came rolling in from the Gulf Stream were as warm in December as on the Jersey beaches in July. Toby, all by himself, swam in the surf and ran on the sand, reveling in the warmth of the sun.

It would have been perfect, he thought, if there had been another boy his own age to share his enjoyment. Once he persuaded his father to come with him, but the doctor had no interest in adventuring up and down the beach. He was content to lie on the sand, soaking up sunshine.

Back to the west of the little settlement there was a wholly different kind of country—the vast, mysterious region of the Everglades. Toby had ventured up the north fork of the Miami as far as the rapids, and followed an Indian trail for a mile or so beyond. From the upper branches of a big cypress he had looked out across an endless expanse of rippling brown grass, cut by twisting water courses and broken by tree-covered hammocks. Some day, he vowed then, he would make a real trip of exploration into the Glades.

Now, mindful of his promise to study, Toby reopened his copy of Caesar and began translating. Dutifully he tried to concentrate on the building of a military bridge. But the scent of orange blossoms came to him from the old tree in the front yard, and the migrating warblers continued their joyful chorus. At the end of half an hour the boy laid the book down.

"I'll finish it later," he told himself. "Right now I've got something more important to do."

He found his father sitting in a rocking chair in the sun. It was good to see him looking so brown and so relaxed. He did less coughing than when he had first arrived, and his gaunt cheeks had filled out a little.

"Dad," said the boy, "I want to take the canoe and see what it's like back in the Glades. How about coming along with me?"

The doctor smiled. "No, thanks. Too comfortable right here. Give me another few months of this, though, and I'll have as much energy as you have. You'll be home in time for supper?"

"Sure, Dad. I won't try to go in very far. Think I'll take the gun along, though, and see if I can bag a turkey. They say a lot o' wild turkeys roost in the hammocks."

Most of the time Toby went barefoot. Now he put on a pair of moccasins and changed his breeches for heavy sailcloth dungarees so tough that a snake's fangs couldn't bite through them. He wrapped up a lunch of corn bread and bacon, stuffed a few oranges in his pockets, and took the double-barreled shotgun from its peg on the wall.

Betsy wanted to go with him, of course, but her mother forbade it, saying those awful Everglades were no place for a girl. He left her pouting in the dooryard and went down to the river. His canoe was there, hauled up on shore. It was an old dugout he had bought with two dollars of the Christmas money his father had given him.

The weathered gray hull was split in a few places, but he had daubed it with pitch and soaked it till the leaks disappeared. It was a crude, Indian-made affair, hacked out of half a log with an adz. The rough tool marks were still visible. Less than two feet wide, the craft was surprisingly well balanced and steady in the water, and Toby was proud of his ability to handle it with pole or paddle. He dragged it into the river and set off up the south fork.

As soon as he left the store behind, he was in the wilderness. Jungle vines grew thick along the bank, and long streamers of Spanish moss hung from the cypresses. Suddenly he heard a musical chattering of birds, and a huge flock of robins settled in the trees by the river. There were thousands of them heading northward from their wintering places in the Caribbean.

The bird migration had started weeks earlier. Toby

had seen pintail ducks migrating first, then the sand-pipers and other small shore birds. The sky had been dark with clouds of red-winged blackbirds over the Ever-glades for days. And now it was the robins, the blue-birds, and the first tide of warblers.

He paddled slowly against the current, watching the banks for signs of animal life. Within half a mile he saw a six-foot alligator lying in the mud beside the mangrove roots. The beast eyed his approach lazily and made no move to leave the spot of sun he was enjoying.

A few yards beyond, a cottonmouth moccasin stirred and glided silently into the river, fat and deadly. Toby had learned a good deal about snakes in the months he had lived at the edge of the Glades. He knew enough to stop instantly and stand without moving when he heard the rustling *whir-r-r* of a rattler in his path. A snake would strike only at something that moved. But with a cottonmouth there was no warning. If you were anywhere near water, you just had to stay alert.

As he went on, the river narrowed for its passage between low cliffs of dark, crumbly rock. Here the current ran faster, and he had to take the pole to push his canoe up through the brawling water. Then he was past the limestone rampart and in a different country.

Before him, as far as the eye could reach, lay a sea of tall, waving saw grass, dappled by the shadows of moving clouds. The river itself seemed to disappear. Only the mouths of narrow creeks among the reeds showed where the water came from. Toby hesitated for a moment over which one to choose, then boldly struck out for the opening directly in front of him.

2

Within a few yards there was no longer any channel with well-defined banks. All that was left of the river was dark water flowing sluggishly through little gaps in the saw grass. Thrusting with his pole, Toby found the bottom shallow—only two or three feet below the canoe—and the pole sank into clinging muck at each stroke.

Now, at the end of the dry Florida winter, the water level in the Glades was low and the saw grass brown and sere. Somewhere far to the west there was smoke in the sky where fire was burning across the marsh.

Doubtfully, Toby chose one of the small water-courses that lay open in front of him and started westward. He had no compass. Soon the only guide he could use was the direction of the sun, climbing the eastern sky behind the canoe. The little creek twisted and wandered and was joined by others. Once or twice the boy found himself in a dead backwater and had to pole his way out, stern first, with the saw grass scraping his shoulders.

It was harsh, unfriendly stuff. Along the edges of the long blades were tiny saw-tooth barbs that could cut flesh and tear clothing. It grew out of the peat muck, and when the leaves died, they dropped back into the swamp to make more peat, as they had been doing for thousands of years. With the coming of spring there were young

green shoots sprouting up at the bottom of the tussocks—
new saw grass that would replace the old.

But Toby wasn't there to make a study of saw grass.
He wanted to move forward toward the distant islands
of trees that were called hammocks. Knowing he would
need guidance to find his way back, he broke a stalk of
grass at each bend of the creek he was following, and let
it hang there like a marker flag.

There was life around him everywhere. Turtles and
frogs plunged into the water at the approach of the dugout. Great blue herons and snowy egrets flapped away on
broad wings when their fishing was interrupted. And
now and then he saw the head of a swimming muskrat
or a water snake.

The sky was covered as if by a cloud, and a vast flock
of red-winged blackbirds passed overhead, their chattering and whistling so loud it filled his ears. For several
minutes they flew over, with smaller groups occasionally
dropping down among the reeds to drink or rest. Then
they were gone, and silence settled once more over the
wide emptiness of the Glades.

Hours passed and he knew it was close to noon, for the
sun stood almost directly above his head. The heat and
glare beat down on him. Even the breeze that ruffled the
tops of the high grass was hot. He tied a bandanna hand-
kerchief around his head to keep the sweat out of his
eyes and kept on poling toward the west, wondering if
he had really made any progress.

Once he heard a gunshot a long way off, the sound
dulled and flattened by distance. Plume hunters, he
thought. They were a sinister lot—renegade white men
and a few Seminoles who slaughtered egrets by the hundreds to get the snowy feathers grown by the male birds.
In New York and Paris there was a demand for those
feathers to decorate ladies' hats. A hunter might get as

much as fifty or even seventy-five cents apiece for fine plumes. Toby hoped he wouldn't run across any of the butchers in his voyaging.

Half an hour later he ate some of his lunch and sucked an orange. Soon, he realized, he should be starting back if he wanted to be sure of reaching the settlement before dark. But he had sighted the treetops of a hammock only a mile or so ahead, and it seemed a pity to have come so far without exploring it. So he poled on through the maze of saw grass.

Suddenly he came out into a little lagoon. Great masses of water hyacinths floated on the dark surface. On the other side, hardly fifty feet away, cypresses and live oaks rose from the bank, their roots in the water and their boughs heavy with trailing vines that made a matted jungle out of the island.

With some difficulty the boy pushed his canoe through the hyacinths. Standing up in the narrow craft and balancing himself with the pole, he looked for some kind of opening in the dense vegetation where he might make a landing. He felt the dugout bump something that he thought was a snag.

Because his eyes were lifted toward the trees, the sudden commotion beside him caught him by surprise. Out of the swirling water thrust an evil-looking snout, and the next instant the head of a ten-foot bull alligator appeared over the gunwale. Scared and shaken, Toby jabbed at it with his pole, thinking he could drive the brute off. Instead it opened its huge, ugly jaws and snapped off the end of the stout oak staff as if it had been a matchstick.

The boy crouched down and seized the gun, which lay in the bottom of the canoe. Just as he straightened up again the alligator gave a mighty thrash with its tail,

hitting the side of the dugout such a blow that it flew right out from under him.

Here in the lagoon the water was deeper. Floundering, Toby went under for a second or two, then came up and started swimming, the gun still clutched in his hand. The canoe was beyond his reach. The hammock, however, was only a few yards away, and he struck out for it blindly, desperately. Now he was almost there. Right above him a big, dark cypress knee stood out of the water, and he made a grab for it with his free hand.

He got his hold and was in the act of pulling himself out when the alligator made its charge. The boy threw the gun ahead of him into the tangled vines on the bank and jerked his body upward. He almost made it. There was a splash below him, and the beast s huge teeth chopped through the canvas breeches into the calf muscle of his right leg.

Toby gave a yell of pain and fear, but somehow he summoned enough strength to drag himself out of reach of a second attack. He lay there, clutching the cypress root, weak and gasping.

Only a couple of feet below him the wicked teeth clashed hungrily, but he was out of reach. The big 'gator grunted and slid back into the water, cheated of its meal.

Toby hauled himself along the cypress knee, working toward the solid ground beyond. Then a twinge of pain in his leg made him look down. To his horror he saw a steady stream of blood dripping from the torn sailcloth. For the first time he realized the full peril of the predicament he was in.

The overturned canoe had drifted to the other side of the lagoon. There was no way to reach it short of swimming, and he knew that meant almost certain suicide. But the wound in his leg was serious. If something wasn't done for it soon, he was likely to bleed to death.

A thin, tough vine dangled within a few feet of him, and he reached up with his knife and hacked off a long piece of it. Then, working as fast as he could, he wound it tightly around his leg just below the knee. With a piece of stick he twisted the rough tourniquet still tighter and felt a growing numbness in his foot as the flow of blood was cut off.

Next he chopped away the ripped pants leg so that he could get a look at the wound. It was a nasty thing to see. He had to grit his teeth to keep from being sick.

It was at that miserable moment that the tangle of vines beside him opened silently and a copper-colored face peered down at him. A young Indian in buckskin leggings and a beaded calico headband stood there looking him over.

In all his life Toby had never been so glad to see a human being. His pale and sweating face broke into a smile, and he greeted the newcomer in the Seminole tongue. Gravely the Indian boy acknowledged the words, but it appeared that Seminole was not his own language. He pointed at the bloody leg, then at the water where the alligator still lay ominously in wait, and he grunted what seemed to be a question.

Toby nodded. He in turn pointed to the canoe, where it floated among the water hyacinths. "Do you have a boat?" he asked.

A gesture of the head showed that the Indian had caught his meaning and was trying to answer in the affirmative. He pointed his finger at his own chest. "Miki-loko," he said. That seemed to be his name. When he pointed at Toby, the white boy knew what was wanted.

"Toby," he replied, speaking slowly and distinctly.

"Toh-bee," the Indian repeated after him and nodded. Then he beckoned for the injured lad to follow him, picked up Toby's gun, and pushed the vines to one side. Limping painfully on his numb foot, Toby hobbled after his new friend.

The path ran only a few yards through the thick jungle and opened out suddenly into a clear space among the trees. In the middle of it were the ashes of what had been a small campfire, and at one side stood a shelter of deerhide laid over a tripod of poles. Toby saw a fish net made of palmetto fibers, two otter traps, and a bow and arrows lying by the tent.

Miki-loko motioned to Toby to sit down. Then, squatting on his heels beside him, the Indian carefully examined the torn flesh of Toby's leg. He felt the tourniquet and loosened it a little, for the whole lower leg was now dead white. Then he went quickly into the woods. When he returned, he had a handful of small, glossy green leaves, which he laid over the wound and bound in place with a strip of cloth.

Seeing the blood starting to ooze again from under the bandage, the Indian boy gave the vine an extra twist around the leg. Then he pulled down the shelter tent, gathered his belongings in his arms, and motioned for Toby to follow him once more.

This time the path—invisible until Miki-loko pulled the vines aside—led toward the opposite side of the hammock. Toby had picked up his gun and now used it as a sort of crutch to steady himself. At the end of the path a dugout canoe was pulled up on the bank.

Miki-loko stowed his duffel amidships, pushed the canoe into the water, and helped Toby clamber awkwardly aboard. The white boy shivered a little as he looked around at the dark water. The alligator's sudden attack was something he couldn't forget. But Miki-loko seemed unconcerned. He poled rapidly around the lower end of the hammock till he reached the lagoon and towed Toby's dugout back to the western side, hauling it out where his own had been.

"Now," Toby thought, "he's going to take me home."

"Fort Dallas," he told the young Indian, and pointed with his arm toward the east. But Miki-loko shook his head. He jerked a thumb in the direction of the bandaged leg, murmured some words Toby couldn't understand, and poled vigorously into a channel that led southwestward.

There was very little Toby could do about it. He wished he could explain that his father was a doctor and would know what to do for the wound. But the sign language they had been using would hardly cover such a complicated idea. From the way Miki-loko was bending his back to the pole, it seemed clear that he understood the need to hurry. Perhaps he was trying to get Toby to his tribal village for help. Or perhaps—and the boy could hardly believe this—he was taking him home as a captive. In any case he was helpless. The pain in his leg seemed less since the leaves had been applied, but he was weak and very tired. He lay back against the rolled deerskin and watched the saw grass glide past.

It was early afternoon when they left the hammock. Drowsing and waking, Toby didn't attempt to keep track of the time, but he saw the sun sink lower and lower ahead of the canoe. Finally it disappeared in the saw grass tops, and the gray of evening fell over the Glades.

Miki-loko kept going tirelessly. He never seemed at a loss as to which channel to pick but kept the canoe moving at a steady four or five miles an hour. They passed a number of hammocks, then as the dusk grew deeper Toby saw a line of big trees ahead. They were approaching a larger island.

Miki-loko pointed at it and smiled, saying several words. One of them sounded like "Caloosa." Then he shot the canoe ahead at even greater speed.

Toby's tired mind tried to make something of the words. Hadn't he heard of a small group of Indians far to the west who called themselves the Caloosa? They weren't Seminoles, but remnants of a very old tribe that had ruled all of South Florida hundreds of years ago.

A moment later they were coming up to the landing. It was a sort of beach, where eight or ten canoes were pulled up. Beyond, among the trees, Toby could see the palmetto-thatched roofs of huts, and the smoke of cooking fires came drifting toward the canoe.

"Ay-yee!" Miki-loko yelled loudly, and at his hail several Indians hurried down to the landing. He started explaining the situation to them even before he beached the dugout.

Two men helped Toby out. His leg had stiffened, and they had to half-carry him up the slope to the village. He was taken into the most pretentious of the houses and laid down on a finely tanned deerskin. A tall, heavily built Indian of forty-five or fifty sat opposite him on a sort of low couch and regarded him in sober silence. From his dress, Toby thought he must be an important personage—perhaps a chief.

Miki-loko entered and stood before the man waiting for permission to speak. When it was given, he told what must have been the story of Toby's mishap, for he pointed at the white boy several times.

Then, to Toby's surprise, the chief addressed him in halting Seminole. Where, he asked, was his home, and what had brought him so far into the Everglades.

Toby answered as best he could, stumbling over some of the phrases he only half-remembered. But the chief seemed satisfied. He gave an order to Miki-loko, who hurried out. When he returned a moment later, he brought two middle-aged squaws with him. One of them was a handsome woman with features much like the Indian boy's. Toby thought she must be Miki-loko's mother.

At once the pair set to work on the injured leg. With deft hands they took off the blood-stained bandage and washed the wound with hot water. It smelled pungently of some sort of herb. Then they brought more leaves and packed them into the lacerated flesh. This time the poultice burned like fire. Toby winced from the pain but kept his mouth shut. All of a sudden his head began to spin, and he remembered nothing more, for he had passed out.

3

The next thing Toby knew it was morning. He roused up at the touch of a cold muzzle on his cheek and was startled to see a small nondescript dog standing by his head. For a moment he couldn't think where he was. Then, looking up at the thatch overhead, he remembered being brought to the Indian village. Evidently he had been moved during the night, for he was in a smaller hut. There was no pain in his leg when he moved it gingerly. The tourniquet had been taken off, but there was no bleeding. He felt rested and well—and he was hungry.

One of the squaws who had nursed him came into the hut just then and saw that he was awake. She chased the dog outside with a well-placed kick of her moccasined foot. The look she gave Toby was as near a smile as her impassive face was capable of showing.

He didn't need to tell her he was ready to eat. She seemed to have expected it, for she carried a half coconut shell that held some kind of food. Toby started to sit up, but she pushed him back with a firm hand. Dipping her fingers in the bowl, she brought out a lump of pasty-looking stuff and put it to his lips.

He shut his eyes and tasted it. It was better than it looked. Coontie root, he decided, pounded to a pulp and thinned with the milk of a green coconut. The squaw continued to feed him, and he ate the whole bowlful. After that she brought him water in a crude clay jar from which he drank gratefully. Next, he supposed, she would change the dressing on his leg. He braced himself to stand the fiery pain, but to his surprise she neither touched nor looked at the wound. Instead she called Miki-loko and left him with the patient.

The Indian boy squatted near him and grinned. In sign language he asked how the leg felt, and Toby managed to convey the fact that it no longer hurt him. Then began a strange conversation. Miki-loko would point at various objects, give their Indian names, and wait for Toby to tell him the words in English. These he repeated as well as he could, obviously committing the queer sounds to memory. Toby meanwhile was learning the Caloosa words.

Quite a number of the Indian names, he found, were like those he knew in the Seminole tongue. Long ago, he thought, before the tribes split up, there must have been a common language with roots that had persisted to that day.

In a way Toby was pleased at the progress they were making, yet he was continually bothered by one thought. He knew that his father and mother must be badly worried by now. Search parties would be out looking for him, and if they found his empty canoe, he would probably be given up for lost. Somehow he must get word back to the settlement. And thinking of that he grew more and more restless.

At noon the squaw who looked like Miki-loko brought him a pot of venison stew and allowed him to feed himself. He ate hungrily and was just finishing the last mouthful when the chief appeared in the doorway.

Miki-loko stood up quickly, and the older man stalked

over to sit where the boy had been. Gravely he regarded Toby for some moments before he began to talk. Then, using occasional Seminole words and a good deal of sign language, he made a formal speech.

Toby couldn't understand all of it, but the general idea was plain enough. The Caloosa, said the chief, were glad that the young paleface had come to their village. It was good that their women knew what to do for the bite of O-kaima, the alligator, and Chitta, the snake. Soon, after two more suns, the white boy would be well enough to go back to his own people. The chief would send his child, Miki-loko, to travel with him to the east, and he would carry gifts, so that the white men should know the Caloosa were at peace with them.

When the chief had finished, Toby knew that an answering speech was expected of him. He sat quiet for a minute, marshaling his thoughts and trying to find the right words for them. At last he began, with as much dignity as possible.

It was good, he said, that the brave Miki-loko had found him and brought him to the village of the Caloosa. If it had not been so, he must surely have died. His father and mother would be grateful to the chief and his people. They would take the gifts and they would send back other gifts, for the palefaces, too, wanted to be at peace.

He had no idea how much the two Indians understood, but the chief seemed satisfied. He nodded soberly, then rose and strode out of the hut at an unhurried pace. Miki-loko also nodded, and his smile showed he was pleased that Toby had mentioned him. They went back to their game and did so well at it that by nightfall they were really able to exchange questions and answers.

Miki-loko was much interested in the shotgun. There were two or three antique firearms in the village, and he went to his father's lodge and brought one of them to show the white boy. It turned out to be an old flintlock musket, long-barreled and heavy. It was so rusty it looked to Toby as if it hadn't been fired in years.

He slept well that night and ate another hearty breakfast. Afterward he was allowed to stand and even walk a little, and he had his first real opportunity to see the Caloosa town. There were, he judged, about eighty people living there. He counted fifteen family houses, and there were a few young, unattached braves besides. From the well-worn paths and other signs it seemed that the tribe had lived in the same place for many years.

He saw cultivated patches of corn and melons and coontie plants, and a number of half-wild pigs roamed about the village. But the main sources of food were game and fish. That morning the hunters came home in triumph, carrying a buck deer and half a dozen wild turkeys killed in the nearby hammocks. For the most part they did their hunting with the bow and flint-tipped arrows, though each man carried a long Spanish-made machete, or bush-knife, for use in hacking a path through the jungle. It would also be a formidable weapon in close combat.

When his squaw nurses made him come back to the hut and rest, he lay there thinking about what he had seen. These Indians were different. He had noticed very few of the kind of trade goods that were so common among the Seminoles. Nearly all their scanty clothing was homemade, of skins, feathers, or vegetable fibers. The few pieces of cotton cloth he saw were coarse stuff from Cuba. And the fact that none of them knew any English words convinced him that their only contact in the past must have been with the Spanish-speaking fishermen along the southwest coastal islands.

That evening he tried to ask Miki-loko about the history of the tribe. But either he failed to make his meaning clear or the other boy didn't know the answers.

Again Toby slept well. When he woke in the early dawn, he was delighted to see Miki-loko wrapping food in green palm leaves and gathering up his weapons and belongings. The young Caloosa grinned at him and motioned for him to get up. This was the day they would travel eastward. Right after breakfast the two smiling squaws took the bandage off Toby's leg. The wound was still an ugly sight, but he was amazed to see how well it had begun to heal.

Almost every Indian in the village was there at the landing to see them off. The chief made a short speech of farewell, which Toby attempted to answer. He thanked them all once more and assured them of his friendship. Then he climbed into Miki-loko's dugout, and the two boys were on their way.

All morning long the canoe moved steadily through the twisting, hidden channels. Toby paddled in the bow while Miki-loko guided the craft with his pole. As far as Toby could see, there were no markers to show the way, yet the young Indian seemed to know exactly where he was going. As they skirted the side of one of the hammocks, Toby caught a glimpse of a young buck fifty yards ahead. The graceful animal was knee-deep in the water, nibbling at lily stems.

Steadying the canoe, Miki-loko motioned toward the gun and urged his companion with silent gestures to shoot. Toby shook his head. His only shells were bird shot, and he knew it would do no more than wound the deer. He pointed to the Indian's bow and quiver of arrows.

In silence Miki-loko bent the bow and strung it, slipping a loop of the tough sinew over the horn tip. Then, just as the buck raised its dripping head, he pulled the feathered arrow back to his ear. *Swish*—it flew straight to the mark. Pierced through the heart, the deer made one convulsive leap and fell forward on the bank.

"Gosh, what a shot!" Toby gasped. "Sure glad I didn't try it!"

They went ashore long enough to skin the buck and wrap up the best of the meat in the still warm hide. Then they resumed their journey while Toby tried to explain why using the shotgun would have been foolish. He could see that Miki-loko was disappointed. The young Indian had a kind of superstitious awe of firearms and had wanted to see this one in action.

It was a good gun—a double-barreled 12-gauge breechloader made in England. The wetting it had taken was not the best thing for it, but Toby had done his best to clean the barrels, hammers, and breech mechanism the day after his rescue.

Just before noon Miki-loko steered the canoe toward a small hammock that looked familiar to Toby. As they drew nearer, he knew it was the island where the Indian boy had found him.

Miki-loko stopped poling a few yards from shore and stared at the spot where he had beached Toby's dugout. "Canoe not here," he said in his newly acquired English. "White man take 'um."

He pointed at the bank, where Toby could see the print of a boot sole in the mud. The Indian pushed the dugout close in beside the bank and studied the signs carefully.

"Two man," he announced, holding up two fingers. "One big, one little. One sun go by."

The mud, as Toby could see, was dry and crumbling around the footprints. If the men were searchers from Fort Dallas and had found his canoe the day before, then his family must indeed be upset.

"Come on," he urged. "Let's get there as soon as we can!"

But Miki-loko was still looking around. He reached out and plucked a tiny wisp of white feather from a twig. "Man shoot big white bird," he commented.

"Plume hunters!" Toby exclaimed. "Maybe they just stumbled on the boat and didn't know whose it was. That means they haven't told my folks after all!"

He was still eager to get home but agreed to rest a few minutes while they ate dry coontie-starch cakes, washed down with Glades water. Soon they were poling through the saw grass once more. After an hour or two Toby was delighted to see one of his broken grass-stem markers. He pointed it out to Miki-loko, and the Indian merely nodded. He must have spotted others that Toby had missed, for he was following the right trail.

As they came out into one of the broader channels, the white boy saw a flock of pintail ducks swimming a short distance ahead. He put down his paddle quietly and reached for the gun. Taking shells from his pocket, he loaded both barrels, then waited while Miki-loko poled slowly forward. They had come within twenty or thirty yards when the birds took alarm. Toby pulled back the hammers, raised the gun, and fired into the midst of the fast-flying ducks. One shot was all he needed. Two of them tumbled into the water.

Now it was Miki-loko's turn to be excited. He poled swiftly forward to retrieve the ducks, apparently even more impressed than Toby had been by the arrow shot that killed the deer.

The sun was low behind them when they reached the eastern border of the Everglades. Pelicans flew over in stately formation, returning from their fishing in Biscayne Bay. Toby directed his Indian friend into the right channel, and soon they were in the current of the Miami, shooting down between the limestone banks.

Miki-loko was wary and silent when they passed the Seminole camping place. He kept the canoe well over toward the other side of the river. Then Toby heard him draw a quick breath of surprise. The houses of the settlement were in sight, and the young Caloosa had never seen anything quite like them.

On the bank at the landing a young girl stood staring at them.

"Betsy!" Toby yelled. "I'm home!"

She shaded her eyes to make sure, then dashed up past the store, her skirts flying, heading for home. As she went by, she must have called out the news, for Mr. Brickell and another man came hurrying down to the landing.

"Where've you been, lad?" the storekeeper cried. "There's men still out searchin' the Glades, an' we'd about given you up for lost."

"It's a long story," the boy told him, "but I'm back safe. How are Dad and Mother?"

"They've borne up somehow—mighty worried, I guess. You better get up there quick."

The two boys hauled the canoe up, took out the venison, the ducks, the gun, and Miki-loko's belongings, and set off up the path. Before they reached the little orange grove, Mrs. Morgan came to meet them, her arms outstretched, her cheeks wet with happy tears. Toby gave her a big hug, then turned to greet his father, who had followed her more slowly. He looked thin and haggard, but there was joy in his face now.

"Thank God," he said quietly. "You're back safe, son."

When the first greetings and embraces were over, the

boy introduced Miki-loko, who had stood stiffly in the background, trying in Indian fashion not to show any emotion.

As they went toward the house, Dr. Morgan caught a glimpse of his son's leg and stopped with an exclamation of shocked surprise.

"That's a bad wound," he said. "Or it must have been bad at the start. Come here and let me look at it."

He was disturbed when he saw the depth of the alligator bite but delighted at the clean way it was healing. Toby told him about the leaves that Miki-loko and the squaws had used, and he nodded.

"I've heard of their herb medicines," he said. "They seem to have wonderful curative properties. I wish white men knew some of their secrets."

Mrs. Morgan had supper ready then, and they sat down at the table, joining in a heartfelt grace. The young Indian was diffident about sitting with them, for all this was completely strange to him. He watched how Toby used his knife and fork and did his best to imitate him, handling them awkwardly at first but gaining confidence as he ate.

Meanwhile, the white boy was telling the story of his adventure from the beginning. He gave full credit for his escape to Miki-loko, who sat there smiling gravely, unable to understand more than a little of what was being said.

When they rose at the end of the meal, the Indian told Toby he would like to make a speech. The family sat down again, and Miki-loko stood before them, tall and straight and dignified, as befitted the son of a chief.

For the first few words, in deference to his hosts, the Indian lad spoke in English.

"Me Miki-loko," he said haltingly. "Me son of Mikko. Mikko Caloosa chief. Mikko and Miki-loko happy help white boy."

That much he must have been rehearsing carefully. He hesitated now, trying to find the right phrases, then switched to his own tongue. Suddenly he was at ease, and even though Toby understood only part of what he said, and the others none at all, they couldn't help being impressed. There was a rolling eloquence in his words.

"We have brought your son Toh-bee back to you," he told them. "He was hurt by the bite of O-kaima, the alligator. In two suns or three he would have died. But the women of the Caloosa used good medicine. Now he can walk again. Soon he will have his strength to run and to hunt.

"This we have done gladly because there is peace in our breasts toward the white men. My father, Mikko, has sent me with gifts to you, our young white brother's father and mother."

He turned to the bundle he had left in the corner of the room and opened it. First he took out three prime otter skins. The fur was glossy as silk, and the skins were not stiff but made soft and supple by the Indians' method of curing. These he presented in turn to Dr. Morgan, Mrs. Morgan, and Betsy. Then from a small doeskin pouch he drew a metal object and laid it in Toby's hand.

"This is white man's medicine," he said gravely. "It was taken by warriors of my tribe from those other white men who came across the big water many, many moons ago. Now my father gives it back to you, Toh-bee."

Toby stared at the thing that lay in his palm. It was a heavy silver cross, four or five inches high. He could see it was of ancient but beautiful workmanship, hammered out of pure silver. Attached to it was part of a broken chain, made of the same metal. And at the center of the cross, where the arms joined the shaft, was an oval of polished, blue-green turquoise.

"Dad," he said breathlessly, "these are wonderful presents. And I owe those Indians such a lot—I'd like to give Miki-loko something he really wants. Would it be all right if I made him a present of the shotgun? We'd still have the rifle, and your old fowling-piece."

His father thought about it for a moment, then smiled and nodded.

"Yes," he said. "I guess I'm glad you feel that way about it. You'd have to give him shells, of course, and show him how to use the gun so he won't blow his head off."

If Miki-loko caught the drift of their conversation, he gave no sign. His face was as impassive as ever when Toby stood up and motioned to him to be seated.

The white boy drew a long breath. "My Caloosa brother has spoken well," he said, in the Indian language. "My father and mother thank the great chief Mikko and his son. Miki-loko has brought us good gifts. We also wish to give something. I have seen that Miki-loko likes the gun which shoots ducks."

Going to the rack where he had placed it, he took the shotgun down and held it out to the other boy. At that Miki-loko could no longer keep his emotions hidden. He sprang up, his face shining with surprise and pleasure, and Toby knew he had made the right choice.

That evening before it grew too dark, he took his friend outside and showed him how to break and load the gun, how to set the hammers at safety cock, and how to carry it under his arm with the barrel pointed forward and down. Last of all he demonstrated how it should be aimed and fired. Miki-loko was an intelligent pupil. He followed the white boy's movements carefully, and when he was finally allowed to try a practice shot, he hit the target.

Toby tried to persuade him to share his bedroom in the house that night, but the young Indian preferred to roll up in a blanket and sleep outside, under the trees. He ate breakfast with the Morgans next morning and then got ready to start his return journey, happily carrying the shotgun and a dozen shells. His parting words were to the effect that Toby and his family must come soon to visit the Caloosa village.

In the days that followed, Toby's leg wound grew steadily better. The bite had left a big, deep scar in the side of his calf, but there was no infection, and as the muscles grew stronger, they seemed to work almost as well as ever.

While he was resting and convalescing, the boy spent a good deal of time with his father. They talked about the Everglades and the strange Indians who had saved Toby's life.

Dr. Morgan asked for a closer look at the silver cross that had been Miki-loko's present to his friend. He examined it carefully for several minutes.

"You know," he said at last, "this silver probably

came from the great Spanish mines in Mexico—a place called San Luis Potosí. I expect some old padre or soldier hammered it out and set the jewel in it. Mexico had turquoise mines, too. How it got to Florida is easy enough to guess.

"Every year—usually in the late summer—a fleet of galleons would set sail for Spain from Cartagena, on the Gulf of Darien. They'd have their holds filled with treasure—Inca gold from Peru—jewels and silver from Mexico. Some of those fleets reached Spain, but most historians guess that half the ships were lost. Many ran into hurricanes and were wrecked off the Keys or in the Bahama Passage. Others were attacked by pirates and looted or sunk.

"When I knew I was coming to Florida, I collected a few books that would tell me about the country down here. One of them has quite a lot to say about this Caloosa tribe of yours. It's the old, leather-bound volume inside there on the bookshelf. Want to get it?"

Toby brought it to his father, staring curiously at the quaint title page. It was called *A True History of the Floridas, as Compounded from Writings of the Spanish Conquerors.*

Dr. Morgan turned the pages slowly. "We'd know a lot less about what went on here in the Everglades three hundred years ago," he remarked, "if it hadn't been for one of those shipwrecks. There was a rich official named Fontenada in the colony of Cartagena. He had a couple of boys, one maybe your age and a younger one, thirteen, and he wanted them educated in Spain. So he gave them $25,000 in gold bullion and sent them off in one of the galleons, in the summer of 1545.

"Well, they were driven on a reef and wrecked in a storm. The older boy and most of the crew were drowned. But the thirteen-year-old—his name was Escalante de Fontenada—managed to swim ashore. He must have been both brave and quick-witted. There were three or four other half-drowned men with him when they got to the beach. Almost at once they were surrounded by savages, who threatened them with clubs and spears and started marching them north.

"The other sailors were stupid. Every time the Indians gave an order, they just looked blank and got a jab with a spear for it. Escalante was smart enough to realize that those guttural sounds meant something, and he had better learn to understand them. By that night he had picked up enough Indian words to obey orders quickly, and he made it clear to his captors that he wanted to know more. So that night and the next day the warriors amused themselves by teaching him the names of things.

"Finally they came to a big village, where hundreds of Indians were living. The white prisoners were led before a tall, hawk-faced chief, who wore a big feather headdress and a lot of gold and silver ornaments. He looked the captives over and asked if they could do anything to entertain him. Of course the poor dumb seamen had no notion of what he meant. But Escalante got the idea. Aboard the ship he had learned a sailor's hornpipe, and he did it now—prancing around and grinning and singing at the top of his voice.

"He could see the chief was pleased, but the fact that the others did nothing made the Indian even angrier at them. Within a few weeks Escalante was the only survivor left. The rest had been bashed in the head for failure to obey orders, or burned as sacrifices."

Dr. Morgan had been turning the pages as he talked. Now he closed the book, smiling at his son.

"Escalante became something of a favorite around the chief's court," he went on. "He grew up with the Indians, and learned to hunt and fish with the best of them.

It wasn't till seventeen years later that he escaped and was rescued by men from another ship. After that he wrote an account of his adventures among the Calusa—that's the way he spelled it.

"You see, that chief was the top Indian in Florida at the time. The Spaniards gave him the name of Carlos, after their own king. He dominated all the Indians in South Florida, from the Caloosahatchee River and the Lake clear to the tip of the Keys, and ruled them with a strong hand. There were two other big tribes that were under him—the Tekesta and the Mayaimi—and they lived in twenty or thirty good-sized towns."

"Mayaimi?" asked Toby. "The same name as our river?"

"That's right. In those days they called Okeechobee Lake Mayaimi. Okeechobee's a Seminole word and wasn't used until two hundred years later. The Spanish sent fleets of ships and armies of soldiers to conquer Carlos and his Caloosas, and were beaten every time. Priests, like brave old Father Luis Cancer de Barbastro, tried to win the Indians by kindness and prayer, but most of them never came out alive."

He picked up the silver cross once more as he spoke. "I was examining this," he said, "to see if it bore any initials. There are some letters here at the bottom—IHS—but they stand for the Latin 'In hoc signo,' that was cut into almost all crosses. I'm afraid we'll never know who owned this particular one, or how he came to lose it."

Toby had sat fascinated by his father's story. "Golly," he said, "I'm glad the Caloosa are at peace with the white men now. If old Mikko had asked me to dance for him, I'm afraid I wouldn't have made out as well as that Spanish boy. What became of all the treasure that was lost in those shipwrecks, Dad?"

Dr. Morgan shook his head. "A lot of it lies at the bottom of the sea," he said. "Millions of dollars in gold and silver, rubies and diamonds, I expect. But the Indians were pretty fair wreckers, and they must have salvaged some of it. Of course, they had no idea of the value of money. The prettier things they used for ornaments. Goodness knows what became of the rest."

He opened the book again. "Young Escalante told quite a lot about the Indian customs," he said, "and some of the stories are pretty interesting. For instance, as soon as he learned the language, he was able to save other Spanish prisoners who were washed ashore just by explaining what the Caloosa wanted them to do. He found the Indians thought the white men were being stubborn when they didn't obey orders.

"What he has to say about their food is really funny, though. He must have kept his feelings to himself and eaten what was put before him, but some of the things they ate always turned his stomach. Perhaps he got used to turtles and alligator tails, but he says they also cooked some kind of animal that looked like a cross between a rat and a dog. It was fat, and it had a long, skinny, hairless tail."

Toby chuckled. "A 'possum, I bet," he said. "Probably he turned up his nose at coontie cakes, too."

That night he lay awake a long time, thinking about Miki-loko and the Caloosa. No wonder they seemed aloof and proud. Three centuries ago their ancestors had been the strongest people in all Florida.

*　　*　　*

By the time he had been at home a week, Toby felt well enough to go exploring again. He had no canoe, so he borrowed Mr. Peacock's old boat and rowed himself to the beach. His father had told him that salt water and the light exercise of swimming might be helpful to his

41

leg. So for several days he enjoyed the surf and the sun,
keeping a sharp eye out for sharks that might be cruising offshore beyond the breakers.

When he got tired of the water, he wandered up the
beach looking for turtle eggs. Twice he saw huge sea turtles waddling down the sand, but if they had deposited
any eggs, he wasn't able to find them. However, it was
on one of these excursions that he made a real discovery. He had wandered some two or three miles northward and was watching the graceful white terns that
sailed and swooped over the edge of the surf when he
heard a strange grunting sound.

It seemed to come from the mangrove thicket on the
inner side of the key. Cautiously he approached the spot.
The beasts that were making the noise might be only a
herd of stray hogs, but he knew that half-wild razorbacks
could be dangerous, and he was unarmed.

As he reached the fringe of mangroves, he heard a loud splashing mixed with the grunts. Through the jungle of roots he could see a pool of water, now thrashed into foam. And in it, playing or fighting, were huge gray-green animals that he thought at first were alligators. Then in a flash he remembered hearing of the "crocodile hole," and he knew he had come upon it.

These creatures, he could see, had much longer snouts than alligators, and when they opened their mouths, they had great rows of ferocious-looking teeth. The ridges on their backs were higher, too, and they were lighter in color.

He watched them for several minutes. Then one of the crocodiles must have seen him or caught his scent, for suddenly every one of them vanished into the dark water.

When he got home that night, his father was much interested in his story. "I'd heard there were crocodiles somewhere around Biscayne," the doctor said. "The only known members of the species in North America, I believe. From all accounts they're fiercer and more active than alligators. So if I were you—after your experience with one of their less dangerous cousins—I'd keep at a safe distance."

5

The next exploring Toby did was along the mainland shore north of the river. He went on foot, lengthening his trips as his leg grew stronger. Because of the danger of snakes he wore heavy shoes and a pair of sailcloth breeches. And usually he carried the old-fashioned muzzle-loading fowling-piece, with its powder horn and shot pouch. The gun had only one barrel and took a minute or two to load, but it was lighter than the English shotgun he had given Miki-loko and just about as accurate.

There was a cart track along the wooded limestone ridge that rimmed the Glades. Following it, he once or twice encountered ox teams pulling clumsy, high-wheeled carts loaded with corn or coontie root, on their way to the mill. The drivers were strange, bearded, weather-browned men in ragged homespun. He could hear the explosive crack of their long-lashed bull whips half a mile away. That was where these backwoodsmen got their common name of "crackers."

Usually, however, Toby's journeys took him away from the road. His great interest was the Everglades, off to the west, and he made his way through the pine and palmetto scrub to the edge of the saw grass. There he

44

would sit for hours watching the thousands of birds that flew past or waded in the shallow water.

There were pelicans, brown and white; long-necked, snaky-looking birds that were known around that part of the country as water turkeys; rose-pink flamingos and spoonbills; and gorgeous scarlet ibis. The big blue herons and green herons were common, too, but it was only rarely that he saw the white egrets. The constant gunning of plume hunters had driven most of them into the farther reaches of the great swamp.

Along the shore he sometimes came upon raccoons washing their food, or sleek otter families at play. Occasionally, toward dusk, he would catch sight of a doe and fawn, coming silently down to drink. And once, walking homeward in the gathering darkness, he heard the piercing scream of a panther somewhere behind him in the woods.

It was some three weeks after his return to Fort Dallas that Toby decided to push on even farther than he had explored before. He took along some food and made an early start. For several miles he followed the wagon trail, then cut over through the woods toward the edge of the Glades, and moved northward until nearly noon.

The sun was hot and he was hungry. He found a spot under a spreading cypress near the water and sat down to eat his sandwiches. For the next few minutes he was too much occupied to look about him, but after his appetite was satisfied he sat back and studied his surroundings. In front of him was a little open cove, merging with saw grass on the west. Just across from where he sat, a point of woods formed the farther bank of the cove. And half-hidden in the reeds there was a dugout canoe pulled up. Then he saw a wisp of smoke rising from the trees. Somebody over there was cooking a meal.

At first the boy was disgusted. Here he had thought himself all alone in the wilderness, and the sudden discovery that he had neighbors was hardly to his taste. Then curiosity overcame him, and he decided to do a little scouting.

Quietly he slipped back into the brush and worked his way to within fifty yards of the place where the canoe was beached. There had been something familiar about that dugout when he had first glimpsed it. Now, after a closer look, he was sure. There was a chip out of one gunwale, and he could see the place in the hull where he had calked a leaky crack. It was his own canoe!

From his hiding place it was impossible to see the cook-fire, but he could make out what looked like the outline of a palmetto shack and catch an occasional movement in the little clearing beyond it. No words were spoken, so it seemed likely that only one person was there.

He was about to move to a better vantage point when he heard the crackle of a twig a little distance off on his right. Then a man's voice called out in a slurring Florida accent.

"Yea, Mose! What yo' fixin' fo' grub?"

"Sow-belly an' yams—like allus. Durn near time yo' got yere, effen yo' want any."

The newcomer chuckled. "Ah ain't been loafin'. Got me a real snowy! Purties' cross aigrettes y' ever seed."

Toby could get a fair view of him as he hurried toward the camp. He was a big, slouching young fellow in a yellow shirt and gray homespun pants, his face shaded by a floppy hat of palm straw. In one hand he carried a gun. With the other he now held up a huge white bird, its long neck dragging on the ground, its breast stained red with blood.

They continued talking after the man reached the

46

clearing, but Toby could catch only the sound of their voices without the words. Careful to make no noise, he crept nearer till he lay in a thicket only twenty yards away. He could see the other man now—a smallish, bearded cracker in a sweat-stained shirt, who bent over the fire and speared chunks of pork onto a tin plate. They ate noisily but with only a word or two of conversation.

At length the one who had brought home the snowy egret leaned back and belched loudly. "Yo' vittles ain't bad, Mose—effen a fella's hongry 'nuff. Ah done heard as how the buyer's comin' through tonight. We got us 'nuff plumes to do business?"

Mose grunted. "Whah's he gwineter be at, Red?"

The bigger man had laid aside his hat, and Toby could see he had a thatch of carrot-colored hair. Now he waved an arm toward the east.

"Over yon'," he replied. "Jack's place. Me—ah aims to git drunk."

"Reckon we got 'nuff plumes fo' tradin'," said Mose. "A jug o' likker'd go good. It's fifteen mile, though, an' rough walkin'. Mebbe we'd bes' git started, soon as yo've done stripped them plumes."

Toby watched while the man called Red plucked the sprays of curling feathers from the dead heron's back. Then he rose and tossed the carcass into the water. At once it was pulled under by some hungry fish or saurian. The plumes were carefully placed with others in a long wooden box, the campfire was stamped out, and the two men picked up their guns. A moment later they had set off eastward through the woods, carrying their precious feathers.

Toby waited until they were well out of sight and hearing. Then he went quickly to the dugout, pushed it into the cove, and got in. There was another canoe there, in better condition than his own. He poled southward through the shallows, and by keeping the higher ground in sight on his left, he was able to reach the upper fork of the Miami by five o'clock that afternoon.

All through the homeward trip the memory of the two plume hunters rankled in his memory. It wasn't just that they had stolen his dugout. They had found an empty canoe with no sign of an owner about, and naturally they took it along. But the whole business of plume-hunting was revolting to the boy. Just because fashionable women wanted feathers on their hats was no excuse for shooting down the most beautiful birds in the Everglades. The less he saw of people like Mose and Red, the better he would like it.

Toby got home in time for supper, and as soon as he had eaten, he went out to do the chores. One of the jobs he enjoyed was milking. He settled himself on his stool with his head against the cow's right flank, wiped her udder and teats, then took the big pail between his knees, and started the rhythmic drumming of the warm, foamy jets into the tin bottom.

When the pail was half-full, a shadow darkened the doorway of the lean-to that served as a cowshed. Looking up, he saw Abel Harris grinning down at him. Abel was a strapping youth of twenty-one who carried the mail up and down the beaches. At the time of Toby's absence and the first few days after his return, it was Abel who had helped his family out.

"That's a right good cow," said the big fellow. "Gives a nice mess o' milk. I come over to see if you could spare a quart for my ma."

"Sure can," the boy replied. "Sit down a spell till I finish stripping. Say, Abe, I got my canoe back today."

"So? Where'd ye find her?"

Toby described the spot at the edge of the Glades.

"Couple o' plume hunters have a sort of a camp up there. I waited till they'd gone off to sell their feathers and then grabbed the canoe. Maybe you'd know who they are. A little chap with a black beard called Mose, and a big young fellow with red hair."

Abel frowned. "Yeah," he said, "I know 'em. Mose Tolin an' Tom Creech—gen'ally known by the name o' Red. Not wuth a cuss, either one of 'em. I ain't surprised to hear they're plum -huntin'. Good thing they didn't see you or you'd ha' been in trouble."

When Toby got through milking, he filled the earthenware pitcher Abel had brought. "When you going to let me hike along with you up the beach?" he asked the mailman.

Abel laughed. "Wait till that leg o' yourn gits stronger," he said. "I have to make thirty or forty mile in a day, so I move right along. Ye wouldn't last an hour at that gait."

He had started down the path with his milk when he remembered something and turned back.

"How'd ye like a dawg?" he asked. "I got one, on'y Ma won't lemme keep him. 'Fraid he'll bring fleas in the house. This dawg follered me all the way down from Jupiter Inlet las' trip. Swum the creeks an' everything. He was awful lean an' I fed him up a bit. Ain't a bad-lookin' animal now. He's a blue-tick hound, like they run foxes with up in No'th Florida. Might make a purty fair 'coon dawg."

Toby had never owned a dog, and he often thought he would like one for company on his rambles.

"Gee," he said, "I'd sure love to have him. If it's all right with my folks, I'll come over an' get him tonight."

Mrs. Morgan sighed a little at the prospect of having more livestock, but she agreed it might be a good thing to have a watchdog on guard at night. As his father made no objection, the boy walked over to the Harrises', eager for a look at his new pet.

As he approached in the dusk, a big, rangy hound trotted out and sniffed at his hand in friendly fashion. Its body was grayish white, flecked all over with slate-blue marks. The long, drooping ears and the muzzle were black. But it was the sad, trustful hound eyes that went straight to Toby's heart. He knelt down and took the dog's head in his arms and rec 'ved a moist lick on the cheek in return.

"Reckon he likes ye," said Abel from the doorway. "He ain't no way 'tached to me, 'ceptin' I feed him. See if he'll go with ye."

"Come on, boy," Toby urged the dog. "You've got a new home."

He started down the path, snapped his fingers once, and the hound trotted amiably at his heels. Abel went inside, and the dog didn't even turn to look back. He seemed to recognize Toby as his real master.

All the way home the boy cudgeled his brains for a name that would fit this new companion of his. It wasn't until he entered the house and saw his Latin book on the table that it came to him.

"Caesar!" he exclaimed. "That's what I'll call you—Caesar. Come here, Caesar boy, an' meet the folks!"

The big hound was undemonstrative but polite. He went from one to the other, his tail wagging gently, then came back to stand beside Toby.

"Well," said Mrs. Morgan, "he seems well behaved, and he looks clean enough. Won't have to sleep in the house, will he?"

The boy chuckled. "No," he replied. "Caesar's an out-door dog. I'm not even going to tie him up. If he likes us well enough, he'll stay here, but he ought to be loose, so as to keep those foxes and 'possums out o' the chicken yard."

He fed the hound some scraps of corn bread and a bone, filled a pan with water for him, and left him there under the orange tree.

The next morning when he came out the dog wasn't in sight, but there was a matted depression in the grass where he had slept. And in a moment he came trotting around the corner of the house, his plumy tail waving a greeting.

When Toby had done the chores and enough studying to satisfy his conscience, he took down the fowling-piece and set off up the road. He didn't need to whistle for Caesar. The hound took it for granted that he was to be one of the party. As soon as they were in the woods, he scouted ahead and on either side, sniffing the scents left in the night by passing animals.

Once he whined a little and looked back at his master.

"What is it, boy?" said Toby. "What you found? Go get 'em, Caesar."

Without further delay the dog put his nose eagerly to the ground and went off at his rangy trot. In a moment Toby heard a mellow baying that told him Caesar was on a hot trail. He followed, keeping as close to the sound as he could, and after half a mile it seemed to stop moving and change to a quicker tempo. As he came up, he saw the hound at the foot of a gum tree and caught a glimpse of a furry ball high in the branches.

Quickly Toby loaded his gun, ramming home a charge of buckshot. The animal had moved a little to a higher limb, but he could see it clearly now—a big raccoon staring down at them with what looked like a grin on its black-masked face.

The boy took careful aim and at the heavy report of

the gun the 'coon came tumbling earthward. Wounded, it was still full of fight when it hit the ground, and it faced the dog, snarling and spitting like a cat.

"Look out, Caesar!" Toby cried in warning. He needn't have worried. The big hound feinted to the left, then jumped in like lightning to fasten strong jaws in the beast's neck. With one quick up-and-down flick he broke the coon's spine.

"Golly!" Toby marveled. "When Abel said you might be a 'coon-dog, he didn't know how right he was!"

6

Toby skinned the dead 'coon and carried the hide home proudly. He was pretty sure he had the best dog in the settlement and wasn't backward about saying so. Before night nearly everybody in Fort Dallas had heard about the hound's exploit.

As for Caesar, he seemed to feel Toby was the perfect master. Everywhere the boy went he followed at his heels. There were times, however, when his devotion was embarrassing. Toby finally had to make a collar out of a tough old harness strap and tie the dog up when he used the canoe. The rowboat was too broad to tip over, and the boy took Caesar with him when he went out to the beach. There the hound's keen scent paid off. He found several batches of turtles' eggs the very first time they explored the sands.

It was about a week later that Abel Harris came to the house one evening.

"How's the leg feel?" he asked Toby. "You ready to try a trip north with me?"

"You bet!" the boy replied eagerly. "Have to fix it up with somebody to do the chores, but Dad promised me I could go whenever you were ready for me."

"Good nuff," the mail carrier told him. "I'm leavin' at sunup tomorrow. Oughta make Jupiter Inlet the third

day. Then another feller takes the pouch up to Cape
Canaveral, an' the last relay goes on to St. Augustine.
You'll be home inside of a week."

"How about Caesar—the dog?" Toby asked. "Can he
go along?"

" 'Fraid not," said Abel. "Fust place, there wouldn't
be room for all of us in the dugout, when we cross the
inlets. An' then we'd have to tote grub for him. He eats
blame near as much as a man."

Toby made arrangements with one of the neighbors
to do the milking and clean the cow stable. The rest of
the chores were light enough for his mother and Betsy
to handle. He went to bed early but couldn't sleep at
first for thinking about the morrow's adventure.

At dawn he was awake, and before he had finished a
hasty breakfast Abel was in the yard. The mail carrier
was barefoot and wore only an old pair of dungarees.

"You better dress the same," he counseled the boy.

"Walkin's easier without shoes, an' you're tanned 'nuff so you won't burn."

Dr. Morgan gave Toby a few dollars before he left. "If your leg isn't up to the long, fast hiking," he said, "you'd better stop off at somebody's house an' pick Abel up on his way back."

Meanwhile, his mother had packed a small canvas sack with food. As soon as Toby had tied Caesar up, he was ready to start. The hound watched them go with reproach in every line of his sad face and drooping tail.

The sun was just rising when Abel beached his boat among the mangroves on the west side of the key. He picked up his own bundle—the precious mail-pouch and some food tied up in a slicker—and Toby slung the strap of his bag over his shoulder. Then they followed the path through the mangrove thicket and came out on the beach.

Abel set a fast pace up the sands. There was a chill in

the air, and Toby was glad to stretch his stride to match his companion's. As they neared the crocodile hole, he found enough breath to ask a question.

"Ever see the crocodiles out on the beach?" he panted.

"Oh, sure. Ever' once in a while I've caught 'em rollin' in the dry sand. Don't git too close to 'em, though. They'd take a leg or an arm off quicker'n lightnin'."

At the upper end of the key there was a dugout pulled up above the tide line. They launched it and paddled across to the next island, then continued northward at a steady four miles an hour.

"It was right along here," Abel remarked, "that I found a piece o' Spanish money last fall. There'd been a hurricane, an' a heap o' driftwood an' stuff had washed in. All of a sudden I came around a pile of it an' there was a doubloon—solid gold—shinin' right in front o' me. It was heavy all right, an' wide as two fingers. Feller at the store give me ten dollars for it, an' I reckon I was cheated, at that.

"'Round noon," he went on, "we'll come to the House o' Refuge that the Gov'ment put up. It's for shipwrecked folks, so they won't die on the beach if they're able to git out o' the water. Mr. Pierce an' his wife keep it. Last year he found an old Spanish chest, all barnacles an' weed, after a storm. He pried her open, an' there was two or three silver coins stuck to the bottom. Prob'ly been full of 'em once."

Toby's right leg was pretty tired by the time they came within sight of the House of Refuge. It was a squat, sturdy building of coral blocks, set well above high-water mark.

The Pierces were a pleasant middle-aged couple who seemed to like their lonely life. Abel was their good friend, for his regular trips brought him often to their door and he was glad to do occasional errands for Mrs. Pierce at the settlements.

She had seen them coming and had the teakettle boiling when they arrived. The boys refused her invitation to dinner, insisting that they had their own food, but she gave them steaming cups of tea to wash it down.

By one o'clock they were hiking north once more. Late in the afternoon they crossed another inlet, and Abel told Toby that what was left of Fort Lauderdale lay over to the westward on New River. Major Lauderdale had been one of the heroes of the Seminole Wars. A few miles farther up the beach they reached a spot that showed evidences of being a camp site.

"Here's where I gen'ally sleep," the mailman explained. "I see somebody's been here since I come through. They caught fish an' cleaned 'em over yon', then built a fire to cook 'em."

With a sigh of relief Toby set down his pack and lay back gratefully in the sand.

"Leg hurtin'?" Abel asked. "I was afraid o' that. Mebbe a night's rest'll fix you up. Trouble is, I got to stick to schedule or the mail's late. You jest stay whar you be an' I'll git the supper."

It was a fine, clear night, and the steady breeze off the sea made it cool, there on the beach. They lay beside the embers of the little fire, and Abel told the boy tales of earlier mail carriers.

"Long John Holman used to do his travelin' at night," he said. "Them days there was some pretty rough characters hidin' out along the coast. Fellers wanted by the law—Confederate deserters—all sorts. They'd cut a man's throat for ten dollars. Long John wasn't 'feared of 'em, but he had to protect the mail. So he'd hole up in a thicket till dark an' walk all night.

"The man before me didn't have the contract long. He forgot to hide his boat at one o' the inlets. Somebody took it—like them plume hunters lifted yours—an' he decided to swim across. Reckon he didn't know the coast very good, because he picked a time when the tide was runnin' out. The current's mighty fast in these inlets. 'Fore he was half way acrost, it took him right out to sea. They found his body on the beach three days later, all tore up by sharks an' barracuda."

"Gee," Toby murmured, "you must have had plenty o' nerve to take over the job!"

Abel laughed. "Shucks, no. 'Tain't so bad nowadays. You take Long John—he had to hike all the way to St. Augustine an' back. I've only got a third o' that. An' if anything happened to one o' my canoes, I'd have sense 'nuff to wait fer slack tide. I figger the job's about as safe as huntin' or fishin', an' it pays pretty good—six hundred dollars a year."

Toby slept soundly under the stars, and his leg felt rested when Abel woke him. They ate a hasty breakfast and were moving again before the sun came up. The boy stuck to it manfully all through that day, but by the time they reached Lake Worth in the late afternoon he could no longer conceal his limp. Every step was painful.

"Look," said Abel, obviously worried, "your pappy'd never forgive me if I took you any further. There's an old feller here that I sometimes stay with. He'll put you up till I come back."

Ten minutes later Toby was introduced to a grizzled, weather-beaten, retired sea captain named Andrew McCosh. Under his gruff exterior the man was both kind and understanding. He lived by himself in a sturdy little house built of old ships' timbers and surrounded by a flourishing garden.

After supper McCosh lighted his black, reeking briar pipe and sat back, eying Toby's leg thoughtfully.

"Maybe I've got a better idea," he said at length. "Sure, I'd be glad to keep the laddie here, but the return journey might be too much for him. There's a schooner up at the inlet with a chap aboard her that's sailing for Fort Dallas tomorrow or next day. A naturalist chap, he is, named Professor Malcolm Evans. Wants to study the birds an' beasties around the Everglades. I'm thinking he might be willing to take young Toby home."

"Yeah," Abel nodded. "But the inlet's a good piece off. How'd he git thar in time?"

"Easy enough," replied McCosh. "I've my own canoe, an' I've no doubt he'd help me to paddle."

"Of course," Toby agreed. "I hate to put you to the trouble, but if this professor doesn't mind, it sounds like a good idea. That way I won't be slowing Abel up on his trip back."

"Well, then," said the old man, "it's settled. I'll wake ye early, an' we'll be on our way."

He was as good as his word. At four o'clock he roused Toby and gave him his breakfast. Then, still in the dark before dawn, they started paddling northward up Lake Worth. At daybreak the pelicans and herons began flying overhead to their fishing grounds.

McCosh may have looked elderly, but he was tough as oak and had amazing strength in his arms. With Toby at the bow paddle, they cut rapidly through the water.

Hours passed and finally they sighted the cluster of houses at the inlet.

"The schooner's still there," said the old Scotchman. "I can see her masts. Verra like, they plan to sail on the afternoon tide. I'll put ye ashore at the landing and wait a bit to see if they'll take ye."

"Whether they will or not," Toby told him, "you've been mighty good to me, and I won't forget it. If you ever get down Fort Dallas way, my folks would like to meet you."

He got out and advanced toward the boarding house that stood a little way from the landing. Looking down at his scanty costume, he could have wished for a shirt and shoes, but it seemed unlikely he could buy them here, even if he had enough money. Two days of sun on top of his previous tan had turned his upper body to coppery brown. Except for his sandy hair and blue eyes he might well have passed for an Indian.

A middle-aged man in a white linen suit was sitting on the porch of the building, writing on a board held across his knees. Mustering his courage, Toby climbed the steps.

"I'm looking for Professor Evans," he said.

The man smiled. "I'm Evans," he answered. "What can I do for you?"

Haltingly, Toby told how his injured leg had given out on the hike up the beach. "I wondered," he finished, "if you could find room for me on your boat. I'd sleep on deck and wouldn't be much in the way. And my father, Dr. Morgan, will pay you whatever my passage costs when we get to Fort Dallas."

Professor Evans looked him over gravely. "How old are you, my boy?" he asked.

"I'll be seventeen in the fall."

"Well, you look fairly able-bodied, aside from the leg. Possibly you could help in the crew. Let's see what the skipper says. He's down there now, ready to row out to the *Pilgrim*."

They walked together to the landing, where the professor introduced the boy to a small, wiry Bahama Negro, wearing the cap of a ship's officer.

"Captain Dunn," he said, "this is Toby Morgan, a friend of mine who wants to get to Fort Dallas. Think you could use him?"

"I take it he's not a sailor," the captain replied in a clipped British accent.

"No," said Toby truthfully. "I'd sure like to learn, though."

Dunn grinned at the professor. "I'm willing to give the lad a taste of sailoring," he said. "It's a short voyage. With a good wind we should be there in twenty-four hours. Will you be ready to sail at two, sir?"

Professor Evans nodded. "I believe the ladies have done their packing. I have a letter to finish before the northbound mail departs, but we'll see you here at one-thirty."

The two-masted schooner *Pilgrim* was anchored a hundred yards from shore. She was neat and trim-looking, with a freshly painted black hull, fresh canvas, and taut rigging.

"We'll go out to her now," said the skipper. "Let's see how you handle the oars."

Toby sprang into the dinghy and rowed with a will, while the little Negro watched approvingly from the stern thwart.

"You don't talk like one o' these piney-woods chaps," he observed. "Are you from the North?"

Toby replied that he was, and explained why they had come to Florida. Captain Dunn seemed impressed when he heard the boy's father was an educated man and a doctor. As soon as they reached the schooner's side, he swarmed up the little ladder and made the dinghy fast. Then he proudly showed Toby over the craft.

There were two other members of the crew, one a huge, smiling Negro from the Bahamas, the other a Key West "conch" whose swarthy skin and broken English showed his Cuban ancestry. Dunn owned the schooner, it appeared, and was sailing her under contract to Harvard University, which had financed Professor Evans' expedition.

Shortly after noon Toby was given a tin pannikin of "scouse." It turned out to be a fish stew, with onions and soaked hardtack to give it body. He was sitting in the shade of the foremast enjoying its flavor when a tall, half-naked figure came striding up to the boarding house from the direction of the beach. It was Abel.

Toby stood up and waved, and the mailman saw his signal. Though it was too far to do any talking, the boy pointed at the schooner, then gestured toward the south, and he could see that Abel understood.

Half an hour later, with the professor's letter added to those in his pouch, the young mail carrier paddled across Lake Worth Inlet to resume his journey.

The tide was full now, and the schooner swung gently about as the current started to run seaward. Captain Dunn sent his big mate ashore with the dinghy. Promptly at one-thirty a party of three people came down to the landing, and Toby looked at them curiously. He recognized the professor. The frail-looking woman who carried a parasol to keep off the sun must be his wife. And there was one other—a dark-haired girl about his own age. Even at that distance he could hear her merry laughter as she sprang into the boat.

7

Toby hurried to the other side of the deck house and tried to make himself presentable. He had no comb in his pocket but he ran his fingers through his tangled hair and dusted the beach sand off his dungarees. A moment later the passengers were coming aboard.

"We've got a new hand in the crew," he heard the professor saying. "Where is he, Captain?"

Before Dunn could answer the boy stepped out where they could see him.

"Ah, here he is," said the naturalist with a smile. "Mrs. Evans, meet Toby Morgan. We're taking him back to his home in Fort Dallas. And this, Toby, is my daughter Susanna, more commonly known as Sue."

Toby had bowed politely to the pale, delicate woman with the parasol. Now he found his hand firmly gripped by the slim brown one that the girl held out to him, and he was looking into a pair of sparkling dark eyes that frankly appraised him.

"Man the windlass," Captain Dunn ordered at that moment. Glad of an excuse to break away, Toby joined the conch sailor at the capstan, and they hauled the anchor cable in. Meanwhile, the powerful mate was hoisting the foresail with a little help from the skipper.

Within four or five minutes the anchor was catted,

main and foresails set, and the main jib in place. With the captain at the wheel they tacked down the channel and cut into the Gulf Stream. As soon as they were well beyond the reefs, the schooner headed south on a long reach, with the trade wind blowing fresh abeam.

Aside from trimming the sheets there was little for the crew to do, and Toby perched himself on the windward rail, watching the blue water flash past and cream into foam in the vessel's wake. Shortly he was joined there by Sue Evans. To his astonishment she had changed from her full-skirted dress to a man's shirt and a pair of dungarees.

"I expect you're shocked," she laughed. "Of course, it's most unladylike, as Mother says. But if I'm going to help Dad hunt his birds and animals in the jungle, she'll just have to get used to it. Tell me, Toby—I understand you were bitten by a real alligator!"

"It was pretty stupid of me," the boy apologized. "Next time I'll know better. My canoe must have run into him when he was napping, and he went crazy. Mostly alligators don't attack people or boats. Are you really going into the woods with your father?"

"Certainly. I've done it lots of times in New England. I can shoot, too, but helping him with the camera is my main job."

"You mean he takes pictures of wild things?"

She nodded. "It's a new idea of his. All the old naturalists, like Audubon and Wilson, had to shoot the birds or animals and then draw them. That's why they didn't always look very lifelike. Dad thinks the best way is to catch them in real pictures. He has a special camera that only weighs about thirty pounds, even with the tripod. It's faster than the ones they used in the war, though of course you can't get a clear photograph unless the subject is sitting still. Some day, Dad thinks, they'll have

64

the process perfected so you can take pictures of a running horse or a flying gull!"

"Gosh!" said Toby. "Your father must know a lot about photography."

"He does," she replied. "During the war he helped Mr. Matthew Brady make some of those wonderful pictures on the battlefields. Then he began experimenting with nature subjects. Last year he got a whole series of photographs of a robin building her nest. That convinced the people at Harvard—and here we are!"

"I'm glad," Toby told her wholeheartedly. "I hope you'll like it around Biscayne Bay. I've been in the Everglades, an' maybe I can help guide your father. I've got a good dog, too, if he wants to run down a fox or tree a 'coon. We could put you up at our house until you find a place to live, and Mother'll sure be tickled to have a northern lady to talk to."

They would have chatted there all afternoon if Mrs. Evans had not asked her daughter to return to the cabin. At about the same time the mate sent Toby forward to haul the jib sheet, and he didn't see the girl again till evening.

The schooner kept the low shore line in sight on the starboard beam and logged a steady six knots despite the northward push of the Gulf Stream current. At sunset they were opposite the place on the coast where Toby and Abel had spent their first night. As the twilight deepened, the captain gave orders to shorten sail. Cruising slowly, they would be off Cape Florida by morning.

Toby was picking out a place on the forward deck where he could lie down for the night when Sue Evans appeared out of the darkness.

"What a sky full of stars!" she sighed. "It's so beautiful I just couldn't stay in the cabin. Are all the nights like this in Florida?"

Toby chuckled. "If you stay long enough," he told her, "you'll see some tropical storms that'll make your hair stand on end. Most o' the time it's nice, though. How much time does your father plan to spend at Fort Dallas?"

"All winter, I expect. He wants to see the fall and spring bird migrations. I told him about your offer to guide us, and I think he's interested. He says he'd like to get into the Everglades—see if he can get some photographs of primitive Indian tribes. I suppose all you see are the Seminoles?"

"Well," Toby told her, "there are plenty o' them around. But one o' my best friends is a Caloosa—Mikiloko. I guess the Caloosa are what you'd call primitive. Anyhow, they still use bows an' arrows."

At her urging he told her how the chief's son had saved his life and taken him to the tribal village. "I reckon I could find my way back there," he said. "Don't know how they'd take to being photographed, but they're friendly enough."

After a few minutes the girl said goodnight, and Toby stretched himself on the cool deck. The creak of the cordage lulled him to sleep.

The big mate roused him at the first sign of dawn. It was still too dark to see the coast line, but the schooner was now running westward before the wind. She held that course for the next hour, and when the sun rose, the broad opening into Biscayne Bay lay directly ahead.

When they moored at Fort Dallas, Toby tried to give Captain Dunn money for his passage, but the little skipper would have none of it.

"You've earned your way," he told the boy. "Give me two voyages, or maybe three, to Nassau, and I'd make a fair seaman of you."

The unloading of Professor Evans' equipment would

66

take some hours, so Toby went home. His parents were surprised to see him returning so soon but glad he had had sense enough to turn back when he found the going too tough for his leg. Mrs. Morgan set off at once to welcome their new neighbors.

"They seem like very nice people," she reported on her return. "I don't think Mrs. Evans is a bit well, and I'm afraid this heat will be too much for her. I hoped they'd come here for a few days, but they've already taken rooms at Peacock's until they can get a house."

"Did you—er—see the daughter?" Toby couldn't help asking.

His mother glanced at him and smiled a little. "Yes," she replied. "A pretty child, but rather spoiled, I'd say. Seems to get her own way without much trouble."

Much as he wanted to speak in the girl's defense, Toby kept his mouth shut. He went outside where Caesar was waiting for him and took the hound for a run in the woods. When he got home that afternoon, he was surprised to hear female voices talking and laughing in the living room. His mother and Betsy sometimes chattered like that, but this time there was a third voice.

"Hello, Toby," Sue greeted him as he entered. "I came over to see where you live. Only Mother said I'd have to dress like a lady if I went calling."

She looked as he had first seen her at Lake Worth Inlet—demure in organdy flounces and even wearing white gloves. He could see that Betsy was tremendously impressed. She couldn't keep her admiring eyes off this elegant stranger.

"I was telling Mrs. Morgan," Sue continued politely, "I expect both my father and mother will be over to call this evening. Dad's anxious to hear more about the Everglades."

She stayed for a cup of tea, then tripped daintily off

down the path to the landing. Toby didn't know what to make of her. Women were a queer lot, he decided. He liked the tomboy in dungarees better.

The naturalist and his wife came that night as promised, and the girl was with them. Mrs. Evans looked better already, Toby thought. Perhaps the long trip south had tired her. His father assured the lady that the summer climate of the Florida East Coast was far more comfortable than most Northerners expected.

"There's almost always a breeze off the sea," he explained. "And with plenty of shade you'll be able to rest and keep cool. I suggest you try some of our fresh fruits in your diet, too. They seem to have helped my own condition."

The professor talked about his expedition. "I'll have my equipment set up for developing plates in a few days," he said. "Then if this young man will be good enough to guide me, I'd like to begin my work. I've heard there are a few specimens of the rare American crocodile to be found in the neighborhood. That might be a good place to start."

"Fine!" said Toby. "I can take you right to the crocodile hole. It's not far—just a little way up the beach."

The naturalist rubbed his hands with delight. "I should be ready by Wednesday," he said. "Of course I'll want the light behind the camera. What time of day would be best?"

"Morning," Dr. Morgan put in. "You can't get close to them except from the east. Isn't that right, son?"

Toby nodded. "The other side's solid with mangrove. But Abel's seen 'em come out on the sand. Maybe we could stir 'em up a little and get 'em in front of the camera."

"Well," his father replied doubtfully, "don't take any

chances. You'd better have the rifle along. Those fellows are dangerous."

*   *   *

Toby waited eagerly for Wednesday to come. He cleaned and oiled his father's Winchester rifle and made one preliminary trip to the beach, taking Caesar with him. The day was cloudy, and no crocodiles were to be seen. Even when the boy thrust a long pole through the mangroves and stirred the surface of the pool, he got no response. A shower came then, and he rowed home, dripping and disappointed, through the rain.

Meanwhile, the Evans family had moved from the boarding house and taken up quarters in a big old mansion that stood near the bay shore, half a mile south of the settlement. Toby didn't see Sue again until Wednesday morning came. To his relief the day dawned clear and bright. After breakfast he bailed out the old boat and rowed down to the Evans' place.

The big house stood in a half-wild grove of orange and papaya trees, with two or three tall coconut palms flanking it. A path had been cleared to the shore, and down it now he saw a figure running. It was Sue, barefooted and in blue jeans.

"Hi, Toby!" she called gaily. "Dad'll be ready in an hour. Looks like a good day for our trip, doesn't it? Come in and see the new darkroom."

He viewed the complicated apparatus the naturalist had set up with awe.

"Gee," he said, "all this stuff is beyond me, but there sure is a lot of it. No wonder you had to charter a schooner to carry it. What's become o' the *Pilgrim,* anyhow?"

"Captain Dunn took her back to Nassau. He's supposed

to come in here once a month, though, to see if there's anything we need."

"You seem to be pretty well settled," Toby told the girl. "Hope your mother didn't get too tired when you moved."

"We didn't let her lift a hand," Sue laughed. "She's feeling a lot better already. Here she is, now."

The smiling lady who came into the room took Toby by surprise. She looked far less frail than when he had first seen her, and there was even a little color in her cheeks.

"Yes," she said, "your father's advice was good. I've been resting a lot and drinking fruit juice. Please tell your mother I'd love to see her if she can come down here to call. They've cleared out the road pretty well, so it isn't a bad walk."

Toby left the boat tied at the foot of the path and went home to pick up the dog and the rifle. He was back by the time Professor Evans was ready.

The naturalist was full of enthusiasm for the expedition. He carried the bulky camera with care while Toby and Sue followed with the plate-box and the tripod. When the equipment had been stowed amidships, it was covered with a tarpaulin to keep it dry. Then the passengers took their places, and Toby picked up the oars.

The tide was coming in. That made the rowing easier and carried them northward to the place where he usually landed. As soon as the bow touched, Caesar sprang out and went ranging across to the beach.

"I don't know how good he is on crocodiles," Toby chuckled. "I brought him over the other day, but none of 'em showed up, so I guess he isn't sure what we're after."

They unloaded the camera and made their way along the path through the mangrove. Ten minutes later, as they carried their loads up the beach, Caesar's eager baying came from the edge of the jungle, perhaps half a mile ahead on the left.

"He's found something!" Toby cried. "Let's hurry!"

8

Fortunately Professor Evans was a strong and active man, for he covered the half-mile at a trot, carrying the camera. Toby, with a lighter load, ran ahead and was waiting for the others when they came up.

They could see the hound darting into the edge of the mangrove thicket, then jumping back.

"It's the crocodile hole!" the boy exclaimed. "And he's got one of 'em about ready to come out after him!"

The naturalist quickly set up the tripod and screwed the long box of the camera in place, a dozen yards from the spot where the dog was in action. He was none too soon, for hardly had he inserted a plate when the long gray beast charged out of the mangrove, its huge jaws snapping at the hound.

Hastily Toby loaded the Winchester and took a stand at one side, where he could fire if he had to. Professor Evans was behind the camera, his head under a black cloth.

"Call the dog off," he shouted, and Toby whistled Caesar back.

For slow seconds they all waited, hardly breathing. The crocodile lay motionless, its long snout lifted and teeth bared menacingly. Caesar was quivering and making little whimpering sounds.

After what seemed a long time the naturalist replaced the lens cover he had held in his hand and hurried to put in a fresh plate. Then he picked up the tripod and shifted it ten feet to the left.

"I want a side view," he panted. "See if you can get the brute to turn north a little."

Holding the dog by the collar, Toby moved up the beach a few paces, then released him. At once Caesar sprang toward his big adversary, keeping just out of range, and the maneuver worked perfectly. The crocodile shifted position to face the hound, and once more Toby called him back.

The professor mopped his brow and gave a sigh of relief as he finished that second exposure.

"Great!" he exclaimed. "If those two pictures come out as I hope, it's worth the whole trip to Florida!"

"You want me to shoot him?" Toby asked hopefully.

"No!" cried the professor with a shocked expression. "The species is in danger of being exterminated, as it is!"

But the crocodile had different ideas. Suddenly he came after them, clumsily but with frightening speed. Professor Evans and his daughter snatched up the camera and plate-box while Toby protected their retreat with the rifle. And once more Caesar proved his value. Nimbly he danced in and out in front of the brute, distracting its attention until the party was safely out of reach.

The whole operation had taken such a short time that they were back at the Evans' house before noon. Without even stopping to eat, the professor hurried his plates to the darkroom and started the laborious process of developing them. At Mrs. Evans' insistence Toby stayed for lunch with her and her daughter.

"One thing Father's discovered," Sue told him proudly, "is how to keep the plates from drying out too fast. In the war, Mr. Brady used to have a darkroom in a tent or a wagon right on the battlefield. He'd have to rush the plates there and develop them a few minutes after they were exposed. And when he moved to another location, it took wagons with teams of mules to haul the equipment. Dad knew he couldn't do that in nature photography, so he worked out a plate-box that keeps the wet emulsion on the plates for two or three hours. That way he can have his darkroom here at the house and get them back in time."

Toby came back the next morning, anxious to find how the pictures had turned out. When the professor put the prints in his hand, he was amazed at the results. Except for some blurring of the tail, the crocodile stood out clearly in both of them. Caesar, who had been jumping in and out during the exposures, appeared only as a fuzzy smudge of motion, but in the second print Toby saw himself standing at one side gripping the rifle. It was the first time he had ever had his picture taken and he was filled with awe.

"These photographs have justified all my hopes," the scientist said. "They prove that wild life can be pictured in its natural surroundings. No photograph of the American crocodile has ever been made before, and these prints will be priceless additions to our museum collection—far more valuable than a stuffed specimen."

Toby was pleased. "Then you'll want me to help guide you on some more trips?" he asked.

"Most certainly I will. Let's see, now. I've got the best map of southeastern Florida the government could give me. Why don't we look it over right now and make some plans?"

The map was a large-scale affair prepared by the Army Corps of Engineers. Toby found it very accurate as far as the coast and the inlets were concerned but somewhat vague in the area of the Everglades.

"Here's the Miami River," he pointed out, "and they show it as a regular stream coming all the way down from Okeechobee. From what I've seen, you can't really follow its course through the saw grass. Another thing, they just sort of scatter the hammocks around, hit-or-miss. I know the first one you can find is at least ten miles to the west."

He searched the farther reaches of the Everglades and saw no mention of the Caloosa village, nor any indication of the big hammock on which it was built.

"Over here," he pointed on the map, "is a place I'd like to take you. Have you ever heard about the old Caloosa tribe?"

Professor Evans nodded, and his eyes brightened behind his spectacles. "Yes, indeed," he said. "They played a big part in early Florida history. I imagine they were wiped out, though, in the Seminole wars."

Toby grinned. "They're still there," he said. "The chief's son is my best friend. He saved my life once. And you'd find, if you went there, that they still have all their old customs and weapons."

"Amazing!" the naturalist exclaimed. "We must certainly find a way to go there. But first I'd like to try the beach once more. Those big sea turtles you've told us about should make good camera subjects. After that we can go after the nearby rookeries of herons, pelicans, and ibis. Will you be free tomorrow morning for another row to the beach?"

The boy agreed to be on hand early. When he went home that afternoon, he was proud of his new importance. Guide to a famous scientist! He wondered what his friends back in New Jersey would think of that.

His father and mother exclaimed over the print the professor had given him. "It's a pretty good picture of you," Dr. Morgan chuckled. "You look really ferocious, the way you're holding that rifle. Hard to tell whether you're scared to death or just anxious to shoot."

There were several more expeditions to the beach in the weeks that followed. Twice Caesar's keen scent led them to nests of turtle eggs buried above the tide line. Toby scooped away the warm sand that covered them, and Professor Evans took a close-up picture with a one-minute exposure, so as to get all the details clear.

Finally, late one afternoon, they were rewarded for a long wait by seeing a big turtle come crawling up out of the surf. They kept at a distance until it had reached the loose sand, high up the beach. Then quickly they moved the camera forward.

"It's a female," Toby whispered. "See? She's digging a hole now to lay her eggs in."

"Why—she's monstrous!" said Sue. "Bigger over than a washtub!"

The light was not too good, and the professor took a number of different exposures. Fortunately the turtle moved very little for fifteen minutes. Then with lumbering majesty it covered the eggs with a couple of sweeps of its hind flippers and started toward the water.

"Want a ride?" Toby asked the girl. "Come on—a turtle won't hurt you."

He helped her get aboard the great domed shell while the beast kept on its way, never changing stride.

Sue was flushed with excitement when she sprang off. "Did you get a picture of that, Dad?" she cried. "I'd love to send one home to Boston!"

Professor Evans laughed. "I tried," he said, "but I'm afraid the light was too poor for the speed I had to use."

They found, next morning, that he was right. One or

two of the plates taken earlier were reasonably good, but the one of Sue riding the turtle was so dim and blurred it was hardly recognizable.

*　　　*　　　*

For several days there had been sounds of sawing and hammering down by the riverbank. Now a flat-bottomed boat was beginning to take shape. Toby had a special interest in its progress, for this was the craft Professor Evans had ordered built to use in the Everglades. The work was being done by two old settlers who had come up from Key Largo. They were experienced boatbuilders and knew something about the Glades.

"Think she'll do for us?" the professor asked, when he met Toby one morning, down by the waterside.

"She's big enough," the boy replied. "Ought to be able to carry a tent an' all your equipment. I guess we can navigate the narrow channels, too, with that narrow beam. When do they say she'll be ready?"

"It's a bit hard to pin them down, but I'd say some time early next week. Can you get away for a few days then?"

"You bet, Mr. Evans!" said Toby. "I reckon we'd better try her out fairly close to home first. Then we can make the long trip to the Caloosa town later on, if she's all right for the job."

The man nodded. "Fine!" he said. "I'd like to get a photograph of a caracara and an anhinga, among others."

"Anhinga?" asked Toby. "Don't believe I ever heard o' those."

"I think they call them water-turkey around here. It's a sort of fresh-water cormorant with a long, snaky neck."

"Oh, sure," Toby told him. "Plenty o' water-turkeys around."

He and the professor made a short trip up the river in

the dugout that afternoon. Within two or three miles they found a rookery of roseate spoonbills, and a little farther on they sighted a water-turkey watching for fish from the limb of a dead tree.

Just as Evans was wishing he had the camera along, a loud clatter came from beyond the bend ahead. It was a heavy hammering that kept up for half a minute. Then it stopped and they heard a short, deep-throated cry.

"Wh-what on earth was that?" the professor ejaculated.

Toby laughed. "One o' those big woodpeckers, I guess. The black an' white kind with a red topknot and a white bill. They sure make an awful racket. I've heard folks 'round here call 'em the 'Lord A'mighty.' "

"An ivory-billed woodpecker!" Evans exclaimed in awe. "Hurry—I don't want to miss seeing it."

The giant bird—more than a foot and a half long from his beak to his tail—had started his hammering again when they rounded the bend. The sun was bright on his flaming red topknot, and his great three-inch bill was driving deep into the dead wood of an old tree.

The professor rested his paddle and sat there staring, his face aglow with pleasure.

"They're never seen up north, you know," he apologized. "This is one of the moments I've looked forward to. How I hope he's here when we can bring the camera!"

On the way home they saw a ripple of water close to the canoe and Toby recognized the blunt head of a moccasin swimming alongside.

"Gosh!" he exclaimed. "It's a cottonmouth!"

Hardly had he spoken when Evans calmly reached out his hand and seized the snake just behind the head. Picking up the gunnysack he had brought with him he thrust the fat, squirming reptile inside and tied the mouth of the bag.

"They're mighty poisonous," said Toby. "Weren't you afraid he'd bite you?"

"Not much risk," the professor replied. "He couldn't strike when he was swimming. I'll take him home and see if I can get him to pose for his portrait."

It was three days later that they launched the pirogue, as the boatbuilders called it. At least a dozen people—most of the inhabitants of Fort Dallas—were on hand to see it take to the water, and a silent group of Seminoles watched from the farther shore. Twenty feet long and only three-and-a-half feet wide, the boat was light but steady in the water, and Toby found it handled easily. He had cut and carefully trimmed down several new poles to use in the Glades, and for deeper water he had the paddles from his dugout.

With the help of the men who had built it, they got the pirogue above the rapids that afternoon and moored it securely to the bank. Next morning early they carried the camera and plate-box up to the boat, and Professor Evans set up the pup tent amidships, stocking it with the necessary chemicals. It would serve as a darkroom on field trips.

That very afternoon they gave it its first trial. Sue, dressed as usual in dungarees, moccasins, and shirt, was in the bow. Toby stood in the stern to pole. And the professor, with the camera braced on his knees, sat just forward of the tent. When all was ready, the queer-looking craft moved out into the stream.

They went first to the spoonbill roosting place and exposed two or three plates. The anhinga was gone, but they found the ivory-bill still at work on the dead tree.

"Get as close as you can without scaring him," Evans whispered. "Then we'll wait till he stops drilling and try to catch a picture before he moves."

Toby inched the boat forward, trailing the pole through the water to make as little noise as possible. At last he was only a dozen yards from the base of the tree. Evans held up a warning hand and steadied the camera, aiming it upward at the bird. After a moment Toby heard him whistle sharply.

The great woodpecker stopped drumming and cocked a fierce, round eye in their direction. For the five long seconds that the lens cap was off, he clung there motionless, glaring at them. Then, just as Evans replaced the cap, the bird uttered its harsh, metallic cry and flew off to a more distant tree.

"I think I got him!" the professor exclaimed exultantly. "Tie up to the bank here, and let me do some developing."

When the pirogue was made fast and the naturalist

had crawled into the tent, Sue and Toby went ashore. The ground was low and brushy there by the water. The boy went first, breaking a trail into the woods, and Sue followed close behind. They had gone only a short distance when Toby heard a sudden dry whir-r-r right at his heels.

"Freeze!" he yelled. "Don't move, Sue—it's a rattler!"

9

He had no gun—no weapon except his knife, and that was useless here. Slowly, without moving his legs, he turned his head. The big diamond-back was coiled in the grass, not more than five feet behind him and about the same distance from Sue. The girl had followed his orders. She stood motionless, but her face was white with terror.

"All right," Toby said quietly. "Stay where you are. I'm going to jump an' make him strike at me. I don't think he can reach me."

He gathered himself and leaped forward, and the lunging snake's fangs missed his bare ankle by a foot. In an instant Toby had picked up a stout stick. As the rattler pulled back to coil again, he hit it with all his might —twice—three times—till it lay squirming but helpless. Then, taking careful aim, he crushed its broad, evil head.

He heard the girl draw a long, sighing breath, and she backed away, her eyes still on the deadly thing in the trail. Toby pulled out his knife and cut off the tip of the big snake's tail.

"Fifteen rattles!" he counted. "An' I bet he was mighty near seven feet long! I reckon we'd better not do any more exploring right now. You look as if you'd seen a ghost."

Sue's laugh was shaky, but she tossed her dark curls. "It takes more than a rattlesnake to scare me," she said. "But you're right about going back to the boat. I'd kind of like to sit down."

He offered her the long cone of rattles. "I guess you earned this," he told her with a grin. "It's for doing what you were told. Any time you're outdoors in Florida an' hear that whirring noise, just remember to freeze. A rattler won't strike anything that doesn't move."

She hesitated only an instant, then grasped the ugly trophy with a firm hand. "Thanks, Toby," she said. "I'm not likely to forget."

Back at the pirogue the professor was still in the darkroom tent, and they didn't bother him. When he finally came out, he looked happy.

"The spoonbills didn't turn out too well," he told them. "But the one I really wanted—the 'Lord A'mighty' —is a magnificent picture, fine and clear. What's that thing you've got, daughter?"

She showed him the rattles and told their story, making Toby's part in it so heroic that he blushed.

"Anybody can kill a snake when it isn't ready to strike," he mumbled. "An' I knew I'd be out o' reach before he could hit me. You'd have been proud of Sue, though. She was standing with one foot in the air the whole time."

Two hours later they were back at the mooring place above the rapids of the Miami. Toby had some doubts about leaving the boat there, for he remembered how he had lost his own dugout. However, this was much nearer the settlement, and it would be almost impossible to move the pirogue up there every day.

They carried the camera and plate-box home with them and securely fastened the flaps of the pup tent.

"There's nothing very valuable aboard," said the naturalist. "We'll just have to chance it. The boat itself would be easy to find if anyone took it."

* * *

Somewhat to Toby's surprise, Professor Evans insisted on paying him wages. They were modest enough—two dollars for each day's trip—but at that time and in that frontier country two dollars seemed like a lot of money. He kept it in one of his mother's old teapots. Some day, he told himself, he would use his savings to go to college.

The next expedition they planned was northward, along the edge of the higher land that formed the eastern barrier of the Everglades. Mr. Evans wanted to get pictures of some typical Florida mammals.

"Raccoons and deer shouldn't be too hard to find," he said. "Wildcats, perhaps, and otter, I should think. But what I really want is a puma. You call them panthers down here. What do you think, Toby? Could we get a photograph of one?"

"Well," said the boy, "they're around here, all right. I've heard 'em screaming in the woods at night. Maybe old Caesar can get on the track o' one. Anyhow, it won't hurt to find out."

The boy was relieved to see the pirogue moored right where they had left it. But when the professor untied the flap of the tent, he backed away hastily, fell over a thwart, and sat down hard in the bottom of the boat. Toby, right behind him, caught a glimpse of a pair of gleaming eyes in the dark interior.

He crouched, holding the rifle, and waited for Evans to crawl out of the way. The creature inside was not moving, but gradually the boy could begin to make out its outline. He chuckled.

"It's a 'possum," he told the naturalist. "I wouldn't

waste a bullet on him. Maybe he'll come out if we stir him up a little."

He picked up one of the poles and jabbed at the animal. The moment he touched it, the opossum dropped over and curled up, playing dead. Cautiously the boy took it by the ratlike tail and hauled it out.

"He'll stay like that as long as we're around," Toby said. "You want a picture of him?"

The naturalist examined the animal more closely. "It isn't what you'd call a 'he,' " he remarked. "Look at that pouch! There must be at least six baby opossums in it. If we could get them to come out, that *would* be a photograph worth taking!"

For five minutes Toby tried to induce the young animals to leave the pouch, but they kept as still as their mother. Then, at the very moment when Professor Evans was focusing his camera, the old opossum made a sudden leap for safety. No longer appearing fat and helpless, she reached the bank and scurried into the underbrush before they could stop her.

They had little luck with pictures that day. Toby poled the pirogue for several miles, and after tying up to the bank in a wild-looking spot, they carried the camera and plates back into the woods. Leaving the naturalist and his daughter at the edge of a small open glade, the boy set off with Caesar to try to stir up some game. The hound soon picked up a scent of some kind, and when it crossed a soft spot, Toby found the hoofprint of a deer, still fresh in the mud. Caesar began to move faster now, his deep voice echoing among the trees. The boy had to run to keep him in sight.

He was pretty well out of breath when he saw the deer. It was a yearling buck, its horns just sprouting, and it was coming toward him in long, frightened leaps with Caesar racing close behind. The buck had back-tracked to shake off the pursuit. It was heading straight for the place where the professor waited, half a mile away.

Toby yelled at Caesar as the dog went by. "Come here!" he ordered sharply. "I know, boy—it seems crazy to you. But we've got to let that deer slow down or there won't be any picture."

The hound gave him a hurt, disgusted look and fell back to trot at his heels. Toby had the rifle with him. He decided if the buck came into view again he would try a shot.

Five minutes later he heard Sue's voice in the distance. "Yoohoo!" she was calling. "Yoohoo, Toby!"

He broke into a trot once more and soon reached the little cleared space. To his relief the girl and her father were both standing there talking. For a moment he had been afraid they might be in trouble of some kind.

"Thanks for chasing the deer this way," said Evans. "He's gone on down the shore. Came right past us, but he was going so fast I had no chance to focus the camera."

He sighed. "Some day," he said, "someone will find a way to take pictures that are almost instantaneous—as fast as aiming and firing a gun. I only hope I live to see it."

Sue laughed. "If you're going to ask for miracles like that, Dad, you might as well wish for colored pictures! Think how pretty that big woodpecker would look in color!"

The naturalist's eyes twinkled behind his glasses. "Perhaps," he told her, "even that isn't impossible. Photography is just beginning to make progress. Why, I've heard there's a man in England who's experimenting with some kind of dry plates! If he could make it work, that would be a big step forward."

Toby had sat down on a log, the rifle between his

knees. He was hot and winded from his run. The air felt heavy, and off to the west there was a faint rumble of thunder.

"I reckon you don't want to get the camera wet," he advised them practically. "That buck sure won't come back this way, an' there's a chance we'll get a shower before long."

"You're right," Evans nodded. "Better start back to the boat."

Caesar had been nosing the wind for several seconds. Now, with a sudden whimper of excitement, he dashed away northward along the same trail he and Toby had just covered.

The boy was exasperated. "Come back here, you fool dog!" he shouted. But instead of minding, the hound gave tongue, loud and eager. He wasn't far away, yet his baying sounded sharper and more frenzied each moment.

"He's got something," Toby exclaimed, "and it's not running away! Maybe we'd better bring the camera!"

He picked up the plate-box and the rifle, and they hurried after the hound. Within a hundred yards they saw Caesar. He was jumping frantically about the foot of a good-sized tree and filling the air with short, breathless barks.

Toby saw the animal first. It lay along a limb some fifteen feet above the ground—a great, tawny beast with wicked teeth bared and tail twitching.

"It's a p-panther!" he gasped.

Professor Evans was planting the tripod, his skilled hands moving smoothly and fast. And Sue was there beside him, ready with a plate. Toby marveled at their coolness. But as he measured their distance from the huge cat, he had a sinking feeling. They were too close. One jump and the panther would be almost on top of them.

Calmly, Evans studied the light and adjusted the angle of the camera. There was nothing Toby could do but wait through the dragging seconds and hold his rifle ready. Slowly he pulled back the hammer with his thumb. The click it made drew the cat's attention from Caesar. The fierce yellow eyes turned in his direction, and he saw the extended claws sink deeper into the bark of the limb. For a frightening instant he thought the beast was going to leap.

But the hound was equal to the occasion. Jumping high against the tree and barking hoarsely, he made such an uproar that he forced the snarling cat to concentrate on him once more.

Toby stole a quick glance at the camera. Evans crouched tensely beside it, his hand on the lens cap, his eyes fixed on the animal in the tree. Then the boy heard him counting slowly. He held his breath. Five seconds—seven—eight—nine—ten.

"That should do it," said the naturalist quietly. "Get back, Sue, but don't run. Keep your eye on the brute. Toby, I'm going to take down the camera now, so keep me covered."

The boy waited tensely, aiming the Winchester straight at the panther's left side behind the shoulder. At the first movement he meant to fire. It seemed like an agonizingly long time before Evans had completed his job, but at last it was done.

Sue, with the plate-box, had already backed away to a safe distance. Now the professor picked up the camera and tripod and retreated slowly among the trees. Toby drew a long breath to steady himself and squeezed the trigger.

At the crack of the report the big cat's back arched convulsively and it slipped sidewise, clawing at the branch. Then it fell, somersaulting toward the earth.

The boy yelled a warning to Caesar, but there was no holding him. By the time Toby had put a fresh cartridge in the breech, the hound had sprung in and clamped his jaws on the panther's throat. And in its death struggle the great cat raked his side viciously with its claws.

Finally the beast quivered and lay limp. Toby approached warily till he could make sure his shot had drilled it cleanly through the heart.

"Careful!" called the naturalist. "Are you certain it's dead? I've heard they're sometimes hard to kill—and dangerous if they're wounded."

"This one's finished," Toby told him. "He cut old Caesar up pretty badly, though, before he died. I want to get the dog home so Dad can do something for him. I can come back later and skin the panther."

"Better bring it along with us now," Evans answered. "It's a fine head and skin. Besides, with those thunder-clouds building up in the west, it might be ruined before you could get back. Give me a hand with the equipment, and then I'll help you carry the brute."

Ten minutes later they were dragging the body toward the boat.

"What do you reckon he weighs?" Toby panted, and the naturalist answered with a chuckle.

"I'd have guessed eighty pounds," he said. "But that was before we tried to carry him. Now I'd put it at over a hundred! Anyhow we know how long he is. I measured a good eight feet from nose to tail tip."

The sky was darkening as they poled the pirogue homeward. By the time they reached the Morgan house, the wind was blowing in gusts and the first big drops of rain were falling, to the accompaniment of crashing thunder. Professor Evans and his daughter agreed to stay there under shelter till the storm was over.

While Dr. Morgan cleaned Caesar's wounds and applied iodine and ointment, **Toby** started skinning the panther in a shed behind the house. Sue and Betsy were interested spectators.

"Imagine my brother killing a thing like that!" Betsy exclaimed. "Why, I remember when he shot his first quail, and he was so cocky you'd have thought it was an elephant!"

"Your brother," Sue told her with some heat, "is not only a good shot. He's brave, too. I thought the thing, as you call it, was going to jump on him any minute."

For once his young sister seemed impressed. At least she had no more to say, and he knew that inside she was as proud as any of them. The girls watched intently while he hauled back the skin from the hind quarters, rolling it neatly away from the flesh. At last there was only the grinning head, which he left attached to the pelt.

The rain had stopped when he finished. Professor Evans came out to admire the job he had done. "If my photograph turns out well," he said, "I'd like to send the skin back to Boston to be mounted. Would you take twenty dollars for it?"

"Would I?" Toby gasped. "Gee—I sure would!"

10

The picture of the treed panther was much better than any of them had expected. Although there had been no bright sunlight, the long exposure had caught every detail of the big cat. And thanks to Caesar's efforts the animal had kept almost perfectly still. Only the twitching tail came up as a blur on the print. The black muzzle, the pale patch under the chin, and the drawn-back, snarling lips that showed the great white teeth were all clear and sharp.

The gashes in the hound's side were deep, but under the doctor's medication they had begun to heal nicely.

"I wish," Toby's father told him, "we'd had some of those herbs the Caloosa people use. Most medicines work about as well on a dog as on a human. If Miki-loko comes here again, we must try to get him to show us the plants."

Toby had hoped he might see his Indian friend before now, but knowing how the Caloosa kept to themselves, he supposed the chief had forbidden him to visit the white settlement. Soon, he hoped, Professor Evans would be ready to make the expedition westward to the tribal village.

It was full summer now, and only the trade wind tempered the fierce heat. Back at the edge of the Glades, where the woods cut off the breeze, Toby found it almost unbearable. Daily, each afternoon, the clouds would pile up in the south and rain would fall in a sharp, heavy shower. The water rose in the streams, and the saw grass shot up green among the brown, dry spikes.

All the migratory birds had flown northward long before. Now only the tropical species were left, and since Evans had already photographed most of them, there was little camera work to be done. Toby went back to his books, studying with a new incentive. He had decided that he, too, wanted to be a naturalist. That meant going to college, and he hoped to be ready in another year. At least he would have enough money to take him north, and he could work for his tuition and board.

He saw Sue occasionally, for she had struck up a friendship with Betsy. The younger girl worshiped her, and Toby chuckled to himself when he saw his sister trying to put on the airs of a young lady. His mother, of course, was delighted at the change in her tomboy daughter.

There came a cooler morning in July when the water of the bay sparkled blue under the brisk breeze. Toby saw Sue coming up the trail and decided he had earned a holiday.

"How about going fishing?" he asked her. "I've got a rod and light tackle, and I bet we could catch enough for supper anyway."

"That would be fine," she said. "I just wanted to go to the store and see if the mail was in."

Toby assured her that Abel Harris wasn't due till that afternoon, for he knew the mailman's schedule well. They took the old skiff and rowed out to the middle of the bay, where the girl was soon trying her hand with the bamboo rod.

The bait they were using was strips of conch meat.

Toby had obtained it from old Jack Punch, an early settler who lived in a shack near the Fort Dallas landing. Under the rickety platform that overhung the water, Punch had a "turtle crawl"—a fenced enclosure partly covered by the tide where he kept not only turtles but crabs, conchs, and live bait.

Sue fished for some time without getting a nibble. The old fisherman had warned them that slack tide was a poor time to try, but Toby wanted to experiment. He tested various methods—floating the bait on the surface, putting on a light sinker, and finally bottom fishing. None of them seemed to work.

"Never mind," Sue laughed. "I like just being out here with the breeze blowing and the gulls flying. Who cares whether we catch fish!"

After an hour or two the tide turned and began flowing up the bay from the sea. Following a hunch, Toby rowed southward till they were almost opposite the first inlet.

"Now," he said, "let's change back to a light sinker and see if there are any fish coming in with the current."

The bait had settled only a fathom or two when something hit it hard.

"Lift the rod!" Toby yelled. "Set the hook and hang on!"

The girl was too excited to answer, but she followed orders. She gripped the handle of the rod with both hands, and the frail shaft bent into a half circle as the line sang out.

"Now reel," Toby told her. "He's made his run. We've got to bring him back."

She braced the rod butt in the pit of her stomach and turned the reel valiantly. It was hard going at first, but she gained, foot by foot.

"I think," she gasped, "he's getting a little tired. And so am I!"

"Here—want me to take it?" he asked.

"Don't you dare! This is my fish and I mean to land him!"

Panting with exertion, she worked the struggling fish toward the boat. Toby stood ready with the long-handled net, and at the right moment he got it under the fish.

"Golly!" he exclaimed, when the catch lay flopping at their feet. "It's a red snapper—best eating you ever tasted—an' I bet he'll weigh four pounds!"

"Is that all?" Sue asked with a grin. "I thought I had a tarpon, at least!"

"Oh, a snapper'll give you plenty o' fight," the boy assured her. "I expect the pull he was putting on that rod was twenty or thirty pounds—about all the tackle would stand. Mind if I have a try?"

They caught six more fish in the next hour, all good-sized snappers, but none quite as heavy as the one Sue had landed.

"That was a lot of fun," she said as they rowed homeward. "And we've got enough here to feed the whole neighborhood! Let's do it again."

It was long past noon when they came in sight of the landing, and Toby was about to invite Sue to lunch at his house when she gave a sudden exclamation.

"What are those men doing?" she asked. "Isn't that your canoe there on the bank?"

He glanced over his shoulder, then bent to the oars again, pulling harder. One look had been enough to warn him of trouble. The two men examining his dugout were Red Creech and Mose Tolin.

He ran the bow of the skiff up into the sand and

jumped out, heading directly toward the plume hunters. The small, dark-bearded man looked up, scowled, and mumbled something to his companion.

Creech straightened his big, slouching body. He sized the boy up and chuckled. "Wal, young fella," he said, " 'pears like yo' got su'thin' on yo' mind. Sho'ly 'tain't this canoe of ourn yo're a-lookin' at."

Toby tried to keep his voice calm. "That's my canoe," he answered. "I bought it last December, an' I can prove it by the Seminole who sold it to me."

Backed by his brawny partner, Mose Tolin grew truculent. "Yo' ain't agwine to prove nothin'," he snarled. "Me an' Red found this yeah dugout way back in the Glades. Some'un—prob'ly you—done stole it off'n us."

Toby was about to reply, but Creech interrupted him. "No p'int in arguin', Mose," he laughed. "We're a-takin' the canoe right now, an' ah reckon this young rooster ain't aimin' to stop us."

He stooped to lift one end of the dugout, and Toby, fighting mad now, sprang forward, his fists doubled. He heard Sue give a little cry and caught a glimpse of her racing toward the store, a hundred yards away. Then he was too busy to notice anything but his adversaries.

Tolin made a rush at him, and the boy side-stepped, hitting him a glancing blow that knocked him over into the canoe. The big redhead gave an angry roar. He was within reach of Toby in one leap, seized him in his powerful arms, lifted him high, and slammed him to the ground, knocking the wind out of him.

Gasping, the boy just managed to squirm out of the way as Creech tried to jump on him. He knew, in that sickening instant, that he was far outmatched. These men fought by no rules. He was due for a brutal beating. But he wouldn't quit as long as he was still conscious.

Suddenly, as he struggled to his feet, he heard the

smash of a fist on flesh. And spinning around he saw Abel Harris standing spread-legged above a big, blubbering figure stretched on the ground. The mailman's face was grim, and he was rubbing the knuckles of his right hand.

"Dunno's I should ha' hit him quite so hard," said Abel. "Looks like his nose is squashed all over his face. Mebbe we'd better let your pappy take a look at him."

Toby had recovered enough breath to talk now. "Gosh!" he said fervently, "I'd have been in worse shape than he is, if you hadn't got here, Abel. How'd you manage it so quick?"

"I'd just got in with the mail. 'Fore I could drop the sack on the counter, this young lady here come tearin' up an' tol' me you was bein' killed. Tolin seen me comin' an' high-tailed it for the woods. I reckon this sort o' settles who the canoe belongs to, anyhow."

They helped Creech to his feet and led him, stumbling, to the Morgan house. The doctor took one look at his bloody face and went quickly to work.

"Nose is badly broken," he commented. "I'll have to put in splints, and it's going to hurt. Better hold his arms."

Red Creech was no coward. He winced a few times but took the rough treatment without a whimper.

"All right," said Dr. Morgan at last. "You'll have to breathe through your mouth for a few days, but you'll still have a nose if you keep those splints in."

He looked from Toby to Abel and knew what had happened. "There'll be no charge," he added with a smile.

Creech nodded. "Thank'ee," he replied thickly. "An' you, Abel, ah'd sho' like to have another go at ye sometime. Ah'll agree it was a fair fight, though."

He turned to the boy. "Keep the dugout," he said. "Ah b'lieve yo' story. She's yours."

When he was gone, Toby turned to Sue, who had been standing near. "The fish!" he said. "Let's get 'em before they spoil! And thanks for saving me from the worst licking of my life!"

*   *   *

In the weeks that followed Toby went fishing with Sue several times. She was a cheerful companion and a good sport. But there were other occasions when he went on expeditions by himself. The Everglades still held a kind of magic that he couldn't resist.

It was on one of his trips alone in the dugout that he found the otter family. This time he explored southward, along the rocky rim of the Everglades. He was paddling quietly, looking up at the thick-growing pines and palmettos, when he heard a splash ahead. Letting the canoe drift, he watched the shore and saw a long, sleek animal come out of the water.

It was a full-grown otter, with a body that looked nearly three feet long. Apparently it hadn't seen or heard him, and he sat perfectly still in the canoe as the craft drew closer inch by inch. After a moment the animal turned its lithe body and entered a hole in a log that lay with one end in the water. It was gone only a few seconds. When it reappeared, it was followed by two little otters—sleek black pups that must have been only a few weeks old.

Toby grinned with delight as the cuddly little creatures started playing together like a pair of kittens. They wrestled and mauled each other, showed their tiny teeth, and did their best to act ferocious. The mother otter watched this sport for a little while, then ushered her babies up the bank.

For the first time Toby noticed a smooth slope of clay, a foot or so in width and half-hidden by brush on either side. With a sudden rush the old otter plunged head first down the slide. Her short fore legs were stretched back under her to make the going smoother, and she shot downward like an arrow, diving into the water at the foot so cleanly that there was hardly a ripple.

Somewhat less gracefully the youngsters followed, one on the heels of the other. Then all three scrambled out again and repeated the performance. How many times they did it Toby couldn't count. He sat there fascinated while the animals whizzed down the slide in what seemed an unending procession. And then, all at once, they stopped.

For a second Toby thought they must have seen him or caught his scent. Then he realized that it was something else—something in the air overhead. As he glanced up, huge black wings flashed downward, and he saw a cruel, hooked beak and outstretched talons reaching for the baby otters.

But they were gone. They whisked into the hollow log with only inches to spare, while their mother, changed now to a fighting fury, rose on her hind legs and snapped at the attacker. The big bird caught itself in mid-air and swerved off, flapping to a nearby treetop.

Toby had thought it was an eagle till he saw its long, bare shanks and crested head. Then he knew it was a caracara—one of the fiercest birds of prey in the Everglades.

"Golly!" he whispered under his breath. "What a picture that would've made! If only there was a camera that could take it!"

He paddled homeward, full of what he had seen. And while the daily thundershower roared outside, he wrote down as accurate an account of the incident as possible.

Later that evening he took the paper down to the Evans' home.

"I remember," he told the professor, "you said you wanted to photograph an otter—a caracara, too. Well, I saw 'em both today! Right near town, where we can go with the pirogue. An' I've written about it. If I aim to be a naturalist, I've got to keep notes—scientific observations, I guess you'd call 'em."

Evans laughed. "That's right," he said. "Let's see what you've written."

For several minutes he sat absorbed by the account, reading and rereading it. Once or twice he nodded. When he put it down, he was beaming.

"My boy," he said, "I'd have given almost anything to see what you saw. We can get pictures of the otter family, I hope, and the caracara as well. But the attack you watched—that's the kind of drama Audubon used to paint! Congratulations, Toby! If you're willing, I'd like to make a clean pen-and-ink copy of this and send it to one of the scientific journals. They don't pay very well, but at least you'll be doing a real service to natural history."

For a moment Toby could only stare at him. "Golly," he breathed at last, "my own words in print? And you mean it would have my name signed to it?"

"I can't promise, of course," said the professor. "But they know me, and if I vouch for it as authentic fact, I think they're likely to use it."

Sue had seized the paper and was reading it with shining eyes. "Oh, Toby!" she cried. "It's good! It sounds so real! Now I *know* you'll be a naturalist!"

11

They poled the pirogue to the spot where Toby had
watched the otters at play but saw no sign of them on
their first expedition.

"I doubt if we could get much of a picture in the morning, anyway," Evans said. "The sun's behind the trees,
and we'll need afternoon light."

Toby nodded soberly. "That's right," he said. "But
this time of year we can't expect much of that. Most days
the clouds have begun rolling up by noon—getting
ready for a shower."

The professor scanned the sky. "Yes," he said.
"They've started already. But look—what's that?"

Sailing high against the edge of the piled-up cumulus
clouds was a small black dot. It circled lazily nearer and
took shape. They could see the widespread wings of a
big bird.

"Could be the caracara," Toby said. "And the tree
where he lit yesterday is that one over there. Maybe if
we get a little closer and stay real still, he'll come back
to it again."

Quickly he poled the boat to a spot near the tree,
while Evans got the camera ready. They waited five minutes—ten minutes—watching the soaring black wings.
Suddenly the bird swooped straight down. They saw the

splash as its long legs and extended talons hit the water. Then the caracara was climbing again, with a fat water-snake clutched in its claws.

"Here he comes!" Toby whispered. "He's heading for the tree!"

The naturalist waited till the eagle-like bird had settled on its perch. Then, while it was putting an end to the still-wriggling snake, striking again and again with beak and claws, Evans focused the camera. There was a moment when the caracara remained still, watching its prey for any last sign of life. And in those few seconds the photograph was taken.

"Great!" exclaimed the professor. "I'm sure I caught him—and the snake, too, dangling down from the limb. That was a piece of luck I hadn't hoped for."

He took the plate into the tent and started developing it while Toby poled slowly homeward. The clouds darkened overhead. The first thunder came when they

were tying the boat up, and it was raining before they reached the settlement.

Nearly two weeks passed before they found the otter family at home. Much to Toby's disappointment it was next to impossible to get a good picture of them, for by that time the pups were accomplished sliders. They were in motion every instant, and though Sue was completely charmed by their antics, her father exposed a number of plates without a satisfactory result. When they were developed, nothing showed on the prints but a series of fast moving streaks.

Several times they discussed the proposed trip westward across the Everglades. Professor Evans was still eager to visit the Caloosa town and photograph the Indians in their native surroundings. But with heavy showers falling nearly every day, they decided to put off the expedition. Besides, the season of hurricane weather might be expected any time now.

"We'll go this fall, when it's cooler and we can count on sunshine," the naturalist said. "Meanwhile, I've got my notes to prepare, and the prints to sort and catalog. There are more than three hundred of them now."

So Toby had more time to spend studying. When he got restless, he took the gun and went into the woods, or fished, or roamed the beach. Sometimes Sue went with him. Sometimes he had Caesar for company. And occasionally he went alone.

One August afternoon when the sky stayed clear, he set out about four o'clock to try for some quail. He whistled for Caesar, but the hound was off somewhere on business of his own. Hiking north through the pine woods, Toby was several miles from the settlement when he heard the whistling of bobwhites in the grass of a clearing ahead. He cocked the old fowling-piece and advanced on tiptoe to the edge of the trees. Once or twice he imitated the bobwhite call and got answers. The quail were there, right enough, and near.

Finally he tossed a stick out into the grass. The covey went up, bullet-fast, and he had barely time to get the gun to his shoulder before they were out of range. No quail fell, and though he tramped on for another mile, he flushed no more of them.

The sun was just setting when he turned back. Before it grew too dark, he worked his way over to the old wagon track that would lead him south to Fort Dallas.

Toby was content in spite of having shot no birds. He swung along, enjoying the cool of the evening, thinking of little except the sleepy chirp of birds, the scent of the pine woods, and the pleasant feel of the breeze. There were mosquitoes, but not too many of them. That was one of the surprises he had found in Florida. His father explained it by the fact that there were almost no stagnant pools where the insects could breed. The water in the Glades flowed constantly, and rain sank into the porous sand and coral along the shore.

Without knowing just why, he found the idle current of his thoughts suddenly interrupted. An uneasy sense told him something had changed. Perhaps it was the silence that had fallen over the trail. He stopped and looked back but could see nothing in the deepening dusk.

As he went on, he became surer every moment that someone was following him. Several times he slipped to one side behind a tree and waited, listening. There was no sound—just a growing sense of a presence back there in the dark.

He shouted, "Who's there?" and got no answer. Finally he shook himself angrily and strode on, telling himself it was all imagination. But the prickly sensation at the back of his neck continued.

He was within about a mile of the first clearings in the settlement when the feeling became so strong he could stand it no longer. Stopping, he pulled together a pile of pine needles and twigs in the middle of the wagon road and touched a match to it. Quickly it burst into bright flame. He moved to one side and stared back along the trail.

At first he saw nothing. Then, fifty yards away, he caught the gleam of two spots of light—two eyes that glowed green against the black. They were not more than a foot and a half from the ground, so he knew the animal could not be a deer. For a moment he considered firing at it. Then he remembered that the gun was loaded with light bird shot. If the beast that followed him was what he thought it was, he would be making a bad mistake.

He took a quick stride forward and yelled at the top of his lungs. And in the dim light of the fire he saw a long gray shape leap from the trail into the woods. A panther!

Toby stamped out the embers and went on, forcing himself to walk steadily without looking over his shoulder. It was hard to do, for he was certain the big beast still followed him. Perhaps, he thought, it was the mate of the panther he had killed, and he shivered.

At last he saw the welcome light of a lamp ahead. As he passed the first settler's cabin, the sense of soft-treading paws behind him departed. Sure that he was no longer in danger, he lengthened his stride and was soon in sight of his home.

"What's the matter, Toby?" his father asked as he set the gun in a corner. "You look a bit pale."

"Guess I am, at that," the boy answered. "I'll admit I was scared for a while."

Briefly he told what had happened, and the doctor nodded.

"Panthers are a little out of my line," he said, "but I've heard of things like this. They seem to be curious about people. Sometimes they follow a human being for miles —not to attack him but just to see what he does."

Professor Evans backed up the statement next day. "Yes," he told Toby, "they have all a cat's curiosity, and no fear. I don't believe you were in any danger. But it's probably a good thing you didn't pepper the beast with bird shot. Then it might have been a different story."

Toby loaded the rifle that afternoon and took Caesar up the wagon road till the big hound picked up the panther's scent. The trail led off to the left and northward again along the edge of the Glades. Apparently the cat had left the neighborhood, for the scent was cold and Caesar failed to show much excitement.

*　　*　　*

Several days of good weather made Toby start thinking about the Caloosa trip once more. However, he found the professor would rather delay it a little longer.

"I was talking to Mrs. Egan yesterday," he said. "She's been around here a long time, as you know, and she's seen quite a few hurricanes. They don't come every year, of course, but old-timers keep an eye peeled for trouble in August and September. In another month or so it ought to be safe enough to start."

He let Toby go over some of the notes he had taken describing birds and animals they had seen. The boy was impressed. He found the naturalist had put down every detail—the time of day and the season, the exact location, even the kind of trees found nearby. The food being eaten by the birds was important, too, as far as it could be observed. Toby realized that if he meant to follow in Evans' footsteps he would have to pay closer attention to everything he saw.

About that time they were interrupted by Sue, who came in wiping the beads of perspiration from her face.

"I've been weeding the garden," she said, "and it's hot work. The air feels stuffy today. Why don't we go out on the bay, Toby? I'd like to catch some more of those red snappers."

He agreed with alacrity, and an hour later they were casting at their favorite fishing spot. That morning, however, they had no luck. The water was glassy smooth under a hot and hazy sun, and there was hardly a breath of breeze stirring.

At the end of an hour Sue grew impatient. "It's probably cooler on the beach," she said. "Or in the ocean, anyhow. Let's go for a swim."

"You haven't any bathing suit," he reminded her.

"What of it? I can do better without that long skirt. What I've got on will be fine—just jeans and a shirt."

"Well," he said doubtfully, "it's all right with me. I bet your mother would be shocked, though, if she knew."

Sue chuckled. "These clothes will dry out in fifteen minutes in this heat," she replied. "Let's go!"

They rowed to the lower end of the beach and pulled the boat out on the sand. Ten minutes later they were in the water, diving through the lazy surf.

"Even the ocean is the wrong temperature," Sue complained after a time. "It's like a lukewarm tub. I'd be more comfortable at home in the shade."

Toby laughed. "You were bound to come," he told her. "Now you've got to get dry before you show up at home. We can sit up yonder under a palm tree and see if that's any better."

They found a shaded spot at the edge of the mangrove

jungle and sat cross-legged, waiting for their dripping clothes to dry.

"Funny," said Toby idly. "Look how that haze is climbing up the sky. Maybe the weather'll change and we'll have a breeze to cool us off."

It was Sue who first noticed the birds a few minutes later. "They're all flying in from the sea," she remarked. "Gulls and terns—flocks of them. I wonder where they're headed."

"On across the bay to the mainland, it looks like. But those aren't terns—those little ones. They look like petrels. I always thought they were deep-water birds that stayed way out in the ocean."

"You're right," the girl said with a frown. "They *are* petrels. And I'm sure they've hardly ever been reported near shore. What do you suppose—look, Toby! The sky's all turning a dirty gray!"

He jumped to his feet. "It's a storm and it's coming fast," he told her. "We'd better get moving. Come on! Back to the boat!"

It was only a few hundred yards to the place where they had beached the skiff. But even before they reached it, the first gust of the wind hit them with smashing force. Toby staggered, regained his footing, and grabbed Sue's arm.

"We're too late," he shouted above the scream of the gale. "Waves'd swamp us before we got halfway across. Give me a hand with the boat."

Together they dragged the old craft up to the highest ground on the key and into the lee of a clump of palms. Toby, putting forth all his strength, tipped it over so that it lay with one gunwale propped up by a mangrove root while the other was buried in the sand.

"Crawl under here, quick!" he panted. "It's going to rain bucketfuls any minute."

She obeyed without questioning his order, and he followed her into the makeshift shelter. As they cowered there, they could feel the boat's tough planking rock and shiver under the drive of the wind.

Sue's eyes were scared. "You know what this is, Toby?" she asked soberly. "I've never been in one before, but I think it's a hurricane!"

12

That was an afternoon neither of them would ever forget. The gusts came harder and harder, and the sudden rain struck the key like lances of white iron. It seemed to fill all the air so that, even sheltered as they were, they gasped for breath.

Time no longer had any meaning. Toby, holding the shaking girl with one arm, used the other to hang on to a cross-thwart of the skiff. It actually felt as if the suction created by the wind might drag them out at any instant. And the boat itself! He wondered how long it could stay in that position without being blown away. All he could do was hold on and pray.

It may have been that his prayers were answered. After one especially vicious blast of wind there was a rending sound, a thunderous crash, and the trunk of a coconut palm fell squarely across the boat's bottom. Fearfully Toby reached up a hand, expecting to find gaping holes in their shelter. But the stout old planks were unbroken. The tree was only half uprooted. It had toppled slowly, anchoring the old craft in place.

For hours they crouched there, knowing only that they were still alive. It was so dark they could hardly see each other's faces; yet Toby couldn't believe that night

had fallen. The storm had simply drowned out the daylight. Some time later—he never knew how long—Toby saw foam running past the boat. A new rush of water flooded the crest where they lay. He thrust out a finger, then put it in his mouth. It tasted salty. The seas had risen so high they were sweeping clear over the island. That was when he knew how lucky they were that the falling palm had driven the windward gunwale into the sand and pinned their shelter down. If the waves got no bigger, it could hardly be washed away.

The temperature had dropped as the gale increased. Toby was cold and cramped and miserable, and he could feel the girl shivering as she huddled against him. Finally she spoke, shouting to make herself heard above the uproar outside.

"Toby—how long will it last? I'm almost frozen!"

He didn't know, but he had to answer her somehow.

"Must be about over," he replied. "Feels to me like it's letting up now."

The white lie choked him a little, but a few minutes later he really thought the wind and the rush of water were losing some of their force. Then at last he was sure. The front of the hurricane had passed.

Within moments there was no wind at all. The screaming and battering ceased, and they heard only the roar of the surf and the drip of water off the mangroves.

"Come on, Sue," Toby urged. "We've got to get out and run—shake the chill out of us."

He took her hand and forced her to trot beside him along the wet sand above the breakers that rolled in, mountain-high. Her teeth were still chattering, but the frightened look was gone from her face.

"Does this mean it's all over?" she panted. "Can we start back home soon?"

Toby shook his head. "I guess you saw what the bay looks like," he said. "The waves are a lot too big, even if we could get the boat out from under that tree."

He knelt and traced a circle with his finger in the sand. "Your father showed me how a hurricane behaves," he told her. "Right now we're in what they call the eye of the storm. The outside edge of it whirls in a circle like this—always from right to left. That's why the wind was coming from the east. But in the middle there's no wind. I figure this storm is moving straight up the coast. In a few hours the rear side of it's going to hit us —maybe just as hard as before. Only the wind'll be coming from the west."

Sue looked at the diagram he had drawn and nodded soberly. "I see," she said. "And if it blows from the west, the boat won't do us any good this time."

"That's right," he had to agree. "About all we can do is get in the lee of the mangrove thicket and hope nothing blows over on us. Come on—run! You're not warmed up yet."

It was hard to tell how much of the day had passed, for there was still no sun. But here in the strange, calm center of the storm, there was a pale light that showed them night had not yet fallen. As soon as her circulation was restored, Sue began to get hungry.

"There were some green coconuts in the top of that palm that fell," she reminded Toby. "And you've got your hunting knife. Couldn't we get some of the milk?"

The suggestion was a good one. They found two or three of the coconuts that hadn't been washed away, and Toby hacked off their tops with the heavy blade. The cool, sweet milk was both food and drink.

After that they began preparing for a fresh onslaught of the storm. The boy cut all the palmetto fronds he could carry, and together they braided them into a thick mat. It was a crude thing but big enough to cover them both. Then they chose the most sheltered spot they could find, on the seaward side of the mangrove jungle, and sat down to wait.

By that time it was too dark to see the approach of the storm. Their first warning was a prickly sensation in the air and a swiftly rising rumble that was more vibration than sound. Then the wind struck, and again that wild howling filled their ears. Leaves, twigs, and whole branches were ripped away in the thicket behind them and went flying past overhead.

They pulled the palmetto mat over them and lay flat under the roaring rain. Somehow, drenched as he was, Toby didn't feel as cold this time. He began to grow drowsy in spite of the screaming gale. It was impossible to see anything in the black darkness, but when he put his ear close to Sue's face, he knew from her slow, even breathing that she was asleep.

He lay for a long time, half-awake, wondering dimly what their families must be going through back on the mainland. The houses, he knew, were built to stand hurricane winds, but there would be plenty of worry over Sue and himself. If only they could signal somehow that they were safe! It was while he was trying to figure out a way to do it that he finally fell asleep.

*   *   *

The next thing he knew his arm was being shaken. "Toby! Wake up," Sue was crying.

He struggled to a sitting position, rubbing his eyes. "What is it? What's the matter?" he asked.

"Something's here with us," she told him. "It's alive— it's flopping around!"

It was too dark to see anything, but Toby crawled about on his hands and knees till he touched something that moved. Cautiously he ran his hand over it and felt it quiver under his touch.

"It's a bird—a big one," he shouted through the gale. "A pelican, I think. Its wing's broken. Must have been blown over here from the Glades."

"Is that all?" asked Sue with relief. "It woke me up and nearly scared me to death."

They left the injured bird where it was and pulled the ragged palmetto blanket over them again. Sue soon went back to sleep, but Toby lay for hours listening to the gradually diminishing storm. At last the blackness thinned and a bit of daylight showed between the racing clouds. The rain had stopped.

Toby got up and stretched. The big brown pelican saw him and tried to flop away out of his reach. Bracing himself against the wind that still blew fitfully, the boy walked toward the surf. The tide was out now, and though the waves were still huge and angry-looking, they no longer threatened the higher ground.

On the wet beach he found a strange mixture of debris. There were tree limbs and green coconuts, seaweed and ships' timbers, dead fish—even a man's felt hat, sodden and battered almost beyond recognition.

Toby picked up a couple of coconuts and a small fish and carried them back to the place where they had spent the night. Moving slowly, he approached the pelican and held out the fish. At least there was nothing wrong with the bird's appetite. It gobbled down the food and opened its great beak for more.

The boy's laugh woke Sue. "Good morning!" she called. "It's really over at last, isn't it?"

"Hi," he greeted her with a grin. "Ready for breakfast?"

Again they had a meal of coconut milk, and Sue gathered more fish for their greedy guest. Then they went together to look at the boat.

"Well, doggone!" cried Toby. "That west wind lifted the tree right off her! If we can get her loose from the sand and find the oars we'll be ready when the water's calm enough."

The oars had been under the boat's thwarts and were still there. After a bit of digging nearby they even uncovered Toby's rod and reel, unbroken but looking somewhat the worse for wear. The boy looked over the skiff's planking and could find no breaks.

"Some of her seams are started, though," he reported. "I can see daylight through the bottom in one place. I'm afraid she'll leak like a sieve."

He shoveled away the drifted sand till the gunwale was exposed, and, heaving together, they turned the craft right side up.

"Not much else we can do till that sea goes down," said Toby. "If I knew any way we could build a fire, I'd try to signal the shore—let 'em know we were still here. But I've got no matches, an' all the wood's too wet anyhow."

"Let's take a hike on the beach," Sue suggested. "I'd like to see if anything interesting was washed in. Perhaps there's been a wreck!"

There was no sign of a wrecked hulk on the shore as far as their eyes could reach. But a strange collection of other things lay strewn along the sand. Hundreds of conch shells and sponges had been washed up. There were starfish, rays, and small sharks stranded above the tide. And farther up the beach, near the crocodile hole, they came on something else.

It brought an exclamation of dismay from the girl, for there, grinning horribly at them from the sand, lay a white human skull.

"Don't get worried," Toby chuckled. "He's probably been drowned a hundred years. When the ocean gets stirred up like this, funny things are washed ashore. Hey —what's that over there?"

He was pointing at a square, dark object half-buried in the sand. Coming closer, they could see it was a small chest, heavily bound in iron that had nearly rusted away. Toby dug out the sand around the corners and tugged it loose.

"Look at those barnacles," he said. "This thing's been at the bottom of the sea a long time. Maybe it came out o' the same place as the skull. Ebony, the wood looks like."

"Pirate treasure!" Sue exclaimed. "Well—aren't you going to open it?"

"It may not be so easy, but I'll try."

He found the little chest quite heavy, but he lifted it high and slammed it down on the sand. The rust-eaten hinges broke away, and the wooden lid fell off. Sue sprang forward. Staring into the box, her eagerness changed to disappointment.

"Nothing but sand!" she announced. "I was sure it would be full of gold and jewels!"

Toby tipped it on its side and began scraping out the stuff with his fingers. Near the bottom, the pale coral sand stopped. The rest was black, caked mud. And just as he thought he had removed it all, he felt something hard and round. Stuck fast in the dark ooze was a gold piece, broad and heavy.

Carefully he scraped the dirt from its surface. Then he grinned and held the coin out to Sue.

"It's a real Spanish doubloon, all right," he said. "But somebody got there first—probably a long time ago. All they left was this one piece."

Sue began looking along the beach nearby. "If it came

from one of those treasure galleons," she told him, "there could be other things like this brought in by the hurricane. I hope the next chest I find has something more in it."

An hour's search produced no additional discoveries worth mentioning. Now that the sun was up and the wind had died, it promised to be a fine, clear day. Toby looked at the giant swells that still rolled in and wondered if he dared risk trying to row ashore.

Sue seemed to read his thoughts. "Pretty soon," she said, "I'm going to be so starved I'll try to *swim* across. Let's go back to the boat anyway. Besides, we have to look after our pelican."

They found the big bird waddling along the beach, picking up his own dead fish. The girl laughed. "I guess he can take care of himself," she said. "But if he can't fly, perhaps we'd better carry him back to his friends."

"Humph!" Toby grunted. "With a high sea and a leaky boat, all we need is a big, awkward, busted-up pelican. He'll make everything just fine."

Beyond the last of the mangrove and palmettos, they had a view of the wave-tossed bay and the low line of the farther shore. Toby shaded his eyes, then gave a start.

"Sue!" he cried. "Look—it's a boat!"

She stood on tiptoe to stare where he pointed. "You're right!" she answered. "I can see the sun flashing on the oars—lots of oars!"

"Four of 'em, at least. Must be the whaleboat Mr. Peacock keeps hauled up there by the store. Where'd they find seamen enough to bring her out?"

It seemed an interminable time before the boat was near enough to hail. Sue was jumping up and down with impatience. At last they saw the man facing them in the stern lift an arm in greeting.

"That's my dad!" cried Toby. "And yours is pulling the bow oar!"

The boat caught the hurrying slope of the last wave and came scraping up on the sand. A moment later the two young people were hugging their fathers.

All of them tried to talk at once. No great damage had been done to the houses ashore, Sue and Toby learned. Some trees were down and parts of roofs had blown off. Dr. Morgan told of finding the cowshed demolished and old Daisy mooing sadly in the middle of a palmetto thicket. But most of the talk was about the castaways themselves. Their fathers looked at the boat. Old Jack Punch, who had volunteered with two of his pals to row out to the island, shook his head as he felt the sprung planking.

"Wouldn't git fifty yards without swampin'," he announced. "Leave her here. I'll come over some day an' calk her up."

Toby ran back to the beach and returned with the struggling pelican in his arms. "Got a patient for you, Dad," he grinned. "Broken wing and possible internal injuries. Nothing wrong with his eating apparatus, though."

They launched the whaleboat through the surf, and Toby took Professor Evans' place at the bow oar while his father continued to steer. The broad-beamed boat took the seas well. Within half an hour they had made the trip safely across the bay to the Fort Dallas landing.

13

The next few weeks were busy ones for all the settlers along the East Coast. The old-timers had been through similar times before and went about making their repairs without complaining. Hurricane damage was something you took for granted if you lived long in Florida.

Toby found his thatched roof had held up better than he expected. There were only about half a dozen places where it had ripped away and had to be patched with new palmetto. When that was finished, he set about rebuilding the lean-to where the cow was quartered.

Caesar stayed close at his side through all these operations. The dog, his mother told him, had acted worried from the time Toby and Sue left in the boat. He had run back and forth along the shore, then returned to the house whining and uneasy.

"It seemed as if he could feel trouble coming," she said. "I think if he could have talked, he'd have sent somebody out after you before the storm struck."

Dr. Morgan tried to put a splint on the pelican's wing but had little success. "I expect Nature can do the job better than I can," he told Toby. "He's managing fairly well now. In a couple of weeks the bone will probably knit and he'll fly again."

The gold doubloon found in the old chest was polished and studied by the doctor. It dated back to the late sixteenth century, he decided. It might have come from a Spanish galleon or from one of the many privateer ships that ranged the coast and cruised the Caribbean in the old days. Toby was tempted to add it to his college fund savings, but gave it to Sue instead.

"Sort of a keepsake," he explained. "So you won't forget our adventure. Anyhow, it's as much yours as mine."

August ended and September began. The weather had been clear and fine since the hurricane. There were hot days, but they were tempered by cooling trade winds. By the middle of the month most of the old settlers agreed that the danger of tropical storms was over for another year.

When Toby had completed his repairs, he went down to the Evans' house and suggested that they might plan now for the trip across the Glades. The naturalist had evidently been thinking of it, too, for he was in full agreement.

"You're the guide and outfitter," he told Toby. "Go ahead and make the preparations. I'll be ready to start whenever you are. There's just one thing. Should we take Sue with us? She's a real help to me, and I'm sure she could stand any hardships we might encounter on the trip. However, her mother is upset at the idea of her going among those savages. What's your opinion?"

Toby was flattered by the question, but he weighed it carefully before he answered.

"I suppose you *could* call them savages," he said. "But after the way they treated me, I think she'd be as safe as she would in Boston. She'd be stared at, of course. Most of the Caloosa people have probably never seen a white woman—or, at least, an American woman. She wouldn't be harmed or bothered, though. If she wants to go, I'd let her."

They had a hard time talking Mrs. Evans into giving her consent. In spite of the benefits of Florida sunshine and citrus fruits, she was still a semi-invalid. And it was hard for her to understand her daughter's enthusiasm for visiting a tribe of wild Indians.

"I can't help thinking of the terrible things that happened so near here," she said. "And that was only thirty years ago. It may have been some of these very same Indians who took part in the Indian Key massacre and killed Dr. Perrine."

Toby had heard the grim story from his father. Back in 1838, a distinguished doctor named Perrine had brought his family to Biscayne Bay and moved into a big, fine house on the shore of Indian Key. He was a botanist as well as a physician, and had experimented with the use of quinine for malaria. Here in South Florida he had shipped in the seeds of tropical plants from Yucatan and intended to cultivate them.

It was in 1840 that trouble with the Indians broke out there. A Captain Houseman, who lived on Indian Key, traded liquor for skins brought in by the Everglades natives. When they got drunk on his rum, Houseman threw them in an outhouse, nailed up the door, and left them there for days. Finally, when they were not only sober but half-starved, he kicked them out.

The giant Chief Che-ki-ka of the Mikasuki tribe was not a man to take this insult lightly, even though a sort of half-peace was supposed to be in force at the time.

Che-ki-ka attacked with seventeen canoeloads of warriors. They came out of the Glades in the dark of the moon and waited on the key till dawn. Then, howling like demons, they broke into Houseman's store, drank the liquor, and began killing and burning. Angry because Houseman and his family weren't at home, they took out their rage on the rest of the settlement.

Dr. Perrine's wife and three children·went out through the bathhouse and hid in the turtle crawl. The doctor, after trying to reason with the savages, got back into the house and, when they burst in after him, climbed up into the cupola. There they caught him and killed him.

By a miracle the Indians didn't discover Mrs. Perrine and her children where they lay in the water. The house was burning above them. When they were nearly suffocated by smoke and heat, they got into a boat tied to the wharf and poled and paddled out into deep water. The dense clouds of smoke saved them. Luckily, they were picked up by a schooner, but many on the island had died in the massacre.

Toby thought about it now and shivered a little.

"From what Miki-loko has told me," he said, "I don't think the Caloosa people were mixed up in that. Some of them may have fought with the other tribes against the whites, but they lived too far to the west to be bothered much. About the only outsiders they ever see are Spanish-speaking folks. Besides—those Indians had been pretty badly treated, and you can't blame them for fighting back. We'll be going as friends."

Mrs. Evans still had misgivings, but she agreed to let her daughter make the trip at last. Meanwhile, Toby was busy figuring out what supplies would be needed. They would be gone from Fort Dallas for at least a week, he thought. Food that would keep was something of a problem, but he should be able to shoot some kind of fresh meat along the way. He packed flour, cornmeal, bacon, coffee and tea, sugar and salt in a stout box. At the last minute he would gather some fruit and some fresh eggs.

The professor gave him money to buy gifts for the Caloosa, and he ordered them from Key West. There would be bright cotton cloth, beads, and ribbons for the women; knives and hatchets for the men. Toby bought a box of shells for the shotgun as a present he was sure Miki-loko would appreciate.

By the end of September they were ready to start. Several trips were necessary to carry all the equipment up to the pirogue. There were sleeping bags and mosquito nets, boxes of food, the camera, plates and chemicals, fishing tackle and guns. Evans was taking his shotgun, and Toby carried the rifle.

They had a fine, clear morning for the beginning of their expedition. It had rained enough to give them high water in the Glades, which was something that had worried Toby. He knew the boat would draw several inches more water than his canoe, and it was less easy to manage in the narrow channels through the saw grass.

When everything was neatly stowed aboard, he took the pole and shoved out into the current. For the first hour they were in the eastward flow of the Miami River. Then, so gradually it was hardly perceptible, the river was gone and the true Everglades began.

Sue was chattering like a magpie, delighted with everything. Most of her conversation was addressed to her father, for Toby was too busy to listen to her. He knew he had to find the route through the labyrinth of channels, and even though he had been this way twice before, everything had a different look that morning. Fed by the rains, the saw grass was taller and greener now. He had to feel his way, partly by the sun, partly by the depth and flow of the water.

All the life of the Glades was in full flood around them. Twice the professor asked him to stop while he took photographs. One of them was of half a dozen alligators sunning on the bank. In the other he tried to catch a pair of great blue herons fishing for frogs in the foot-deep water.

By noon, Toby figured they had gone. only about a dozen miles. They had not yet come in sight of any large hammocks, so they ate their lunch of sandwiches in the boat.

"You can drink the Glades water all right," Toby told his companions. "It's fresh an' clean."

Professor Evans agreed that it tasted fine. After twenty minutes they were ready to push forward once more. The boy felt a heavy responsibility for the success of this trip, and he gave extra care to the route they followed. At every turning he broke a saw grass stalk and left it hanging as a marker.

It was about four o'clock that afternoon when he saw the familiar outline of a hammock on the horizon ahead. He was almost certain it was the place where the Indian boy had found him after his mishap with the alligator.

"There's some fairly high ground on that island ahead," he told the others. "It ought to give us a place to camp if we get there before dark."

By the twisting water courses, the distance was greater than it looked. Patiently Toby pushed the boat along, bearing sometimes to the right, sometimes to the left, but always keeping the treetops of the hammock in sight. It was almost sunset when the bow of the pirogue emerged in a narrow lagoon.

The place was just as he remembered it—the floating patches of water hyacinths, the looming pines and cypress trees. Even the alligators were present. From somewhere up the lagoon he heard the muffled bellow of a big bull 'gator—perhaps the same one that had attacked him in the dugout.

"The best landing is over on the other side," said Toby, and he steered the boat southward to skirt the lower end of the hammock.

At that moment Sue gave a start. "Look!" she whispered. "Those big birds flying in—aren't they turkeys?"

Turning his head, Toby got a glimpse of them. "Gee!" he breathed. "That's luck! They're coming in to roost. Maybe we can get one for supper."

They found the landing place and beached the pirogue. The professor got out, loading his shotgun, and Toby hesitated, looking at Sue. Obviously she was eager to go on the hunt, but she shook her head.

"Three's too many," she said. "We'd be sure to scare them. You know the island, so you go with Daddy. I'll stay here and look after things."

The boy led the way, moving silently on the soft carpet of pine needles. Turkeys were about the hardest game of any to stalk. As they approached the roosting place, darkness was falling fast. Toby stopped and listened, and he could hear faint squawkings and gobblings in the trees ahead. They weren't sounds of alarm. The birds were just getting settled for the night.

With Evans close behind him, he advanced a step at a time. At each stride he felt with his moccasin toe for a safe spot to set his foot. A crackling stick would ruin everything. At last he could see two or three blobs of blackness high in a tree, silhouetted against the faint light of dusk.

They were at least fifty yards away, but he didn't dare approach any closer. Silently he pointed to the roosting turkeys, and the professor nodded. He moved into position beside Toby and cocked the gun. At the faint click there was a stirring among the birds and a sharp, questioning gobble.

"Quick!" Toby whispered.

A second later Evans took aim and fired both barrels in fast succession. With a whir of wings the flock took off, but one turkey had toppled from the limb. The boy darted forward, careless now of noise. The wounded bird was flopping in the underbrush, only yards away.

Toby plunged into the thicket and made a grab for it. His hands and arms were scratched by thorns, but he got his fingers around the turkey's leg and held on.

It was practically dark when they stumbled back to the boat. A small campfire was burning there, and its welcoming glow guided them the last few steps. Once again Toby was impressed by Sue's competence in the woods. It wasn't every girl who could build a fire so quickly.

There wasn't time to roast the turkey properly, but Toby plucked and cleaned it, cut the meat into chunks, and thrust them on green sticks. Sitting around the blaze, they held the sizzling pieces over the flames till

they were cooked enough to eat, and all three of them called it a delicious meal.

They laid out the sleeping bags around the fire, feet facing in toward the still-red embers. It was a cool, starlit evening, and the warmth felt good.

Toby was the last to lie down. He made a quiet circuit around the camp to make sure all was well. The naturalist and his daughter had hung their mosquito nets over little frameworks of sticks. The boy didn't bother with a net. If there were any of the insects around, let them bite. His skin was tough.

With the responsibility for the trip on his mind, he had trouble getting to sleep, and it must have been ten o'clock before he finally dozed off. Two or three hours later he woke with a start. Had he imagined it, or was there something moving, close to his body?

Cautiously he moved a hand and it came in contact with cold, smooth scales! Like a flash Toby jumped to his feet, letting the canvas sleeping bag drop away from him. In the faint glow of the coals he saw a snake slither out of the bag and glide away into the brush before he could find a club.

With a shiver he gave the canvas a thorough shaking, but he couldn't bring himself to get into it again. Probably he had been in no real danger. The reptile had merely wanted to get warm. Toby put a little more wood on the fire and sat huddled beside it the rest of the night.

At daybreak Sue woke and sat up, rubbing her eyes.

"You certainly got up early, Toby," she laughed. "Wasn't your bed comfortable?"

"Guess I was just restless," he said, not wanting to alarm her. "But I got enough sleep. No need to wake your father yet. I'll just start up a cooking fire."

Together they fried bacon, eggs, and johnnycake in

the skillet and made a pot of coffee. Then, when Sue had called her father, they sat down to breakfast.

The clear sky promised another good day when they repacked their duffel in the pirogue and prepared to shove off. Toby had little to say, for he was thinking hard about the route ahead. After these months it wasn't easy to remember all the forks and bends in those strange waterways.

He had taken only half a dozen strokes with the pole when he saw a dugout shoot suddenly out of a channel in the saw grass ahead. There was a single figure paddling—a slim, half-naked youth with the bronze skin of an Indian.

"Miki-loko!" Toby yelled with joy. "Where are you headed? We're on our way to visit you."

The Indian boy raised an arm in greeting and swung the canoe toward them. As he pulled alongside, Toby was shocked at his appearance. His face was gaunt and drawn, and his thin chest heaved.

"Caloosa got much trouble," he panted. "Bad trouble. Much sickness. Maybe you come help, Toh-bee."

14

There was no time for introductions. Toby had to find out quickly what was wrong. He still remembered enough of the Caloosa language to ask questions, and Miki-loko did his best to make him understand.

The white boy's face was grave when he turned to his companions.

"It's some kind of disease that's hit the whole tribe," he said. "The sickness of many spots, Miki-loko calls it. What's that sound like to you?"

"I hate to say it," Evans answered, "but it could be smallpox. Or maybe chicken pox or measles. Ask him how sick they are."

"They're mighty sick, all right. He told me two men had died. Most o' the Indians in the town have got panicky and left. Gone off in the swamps away from the sick ones. I guess the best thing to do is get Miki-loko to Fort Dallas as fast as we can, an' let Dad have a look at him."

The naturalist nodded. "Here," he said, "I'll take the other pole, and we can make more speed. Will he show us the way?"

Toby called out to the young Indian. "We go back with you." He pointed eastward. "Aren't you hungry? Better have something to eat first."

But Miki-loko shook his head. He picked up the paddle and shot the canoe forward, past the end of the hammock. Poling hard, they followed him into the maze of the saw grass.

There was no stop for a noon meal. Frail and thin as he appeared, the Indian boy paddled tirelessly, and it was all Toby could do to keep him in sight. At about two o'clock in the afternoon they were in the channel of the Miami and nearing the piney ridge that marked the edge of the Everglades.

At the place where they had made their start the day before, the professor called a halt.

"You go with him in the dugout, Toby. Sue and I'll tie up here, and we can handle the camera and plates. The rest of the equipment we'll just leave under the tent and trust to luck. The main thing now is to get that boy to the doctor."

Toby had to agree. He ran to the canoe and got in, picking up the spare paddle. A few moments later they were in the white water, racing down the rapids. And within half an hour they reached the landing at the settlement.

Miki-loko staggered a little as he got out of the canoe. He must have been close to the point of exhaustion, for he had been traveling since midnight without rest or food. Toby reached out a hand to steady him, but the Indian lad drew away, standing proudly erect. It was part of his code never to show weakness.

Dr. Morgan had been taking his siesta in a hammock under the palms. He saw the two boys coming and knew something must be wrong. He welcomed Miki-loko, then turned to his son.

"What's happened, Toby?" he asked.

Quickly Toby outlined the situation, or as much of it as he had been able to gather from his friend.

"The sickness of many spots is what the Indians call it," he said. "And it must be bad or they wouldn't all be so scared. I don't know whether Miki-loko's got it yet, but you'll want to take a look at him."

The doctor led the way into the house, asking a rapid fire of questions, which Toby tried to translate. Then he went over the Caloosa boy carefully.

"He doesn't show any symptoms yet," he said, when the examination was over. "He's pretty well tuckered out, though, from exertion and worry and lack of food. I'm pretty sure the sickness he describes is smallpox. So the first thing to do is vaccinate him. Will he let me do it?"

Partly in pantomime, partly in Indian phrases, Toby did his best to explain what vaccination was. He didn't seem to be making much headway, but an inspiration came to him.

"Here, Dad," he said, rolling up his sleeve to the shoulder, "why don't you do it to me? That'll show him what it's like."

Miki-loko watched intently while the alcohol was dabbed on the arm, the scratch made, and the vaccine applied. At once he understood. Without hesitation he stepped forward and held out his own arm.

While these things were going on, Toby's mother had been busy in the kitchen. She set bowls of soup, meat, corn bread, and turnip greens before the two boys. The young Indian tried not to show how hungry he was, but he was still eating when Toby had had all he could hold.

Then the doctor came and sat down at the table.

"Son," he said, "we've got to do something about this epidemic. How long does it take to reach the Caloosa town?"

"It's a full-day trip—maybe forty miles," the boy replied. "A white man who didn't know the way would take a lot longer, even if he didn't get lost."

"But you think we could make it in a long day in the pirogue?" his father asked.

"With Miki-loko to guide us, I think we could."

"All right," the doctor nodded. "But first we've got to have more serum. My supply is only enough for half a dozen more vaccinations, and I expect folks here in Fort Dallas will be panicky as soon as they hear of it. Some will be afraid of being vaccinated, but others will want me to do it quick.

"Now there are two places where there may be a supply. One's Fort Lauderdale. There's no Army doctor there now, but it's possible the garrison kept a stock of medicines. The other place—a lot farther to go—is Key West. We might have to wait a week before a schooner that could get it for us comes in here."

"Maybe not," said Toby eagerly. "Mr. Evans said he expected the *Pilgrim* today or tomorrow. You know—the schooner he chartered. I bet Captain Dunn would make a rush trip to Key West. And if Abel Harris is home, he could get to Fort Lauderdale and back in a day. I'll go ask him."

The boy ran all the way to the mailman's house and found him working in his vegetable garden. Quickly he told him the situation, and, as he expected, Abel agreed to go at once.

"There's a moon," he said. "I can make it tonight an' be back here 'fore midday tomorrow. Dunno's they got what you need up at the fort, but I'll do my best."

On the way home Toby saw tall white sails coming into the river mouth, and at the landing he found Professor Evans and Sue. They were waiting for the crew of the *Pilgrim* to come ashore.

When the naturalist heard what Dr. Morgan proposed

doing, he was in full agreement. "We've got to save as many of the Indians as we can," he said, "and there isn't much time. I'll talk to Dunn the minute he lands."

Toby went home to report to his father. "Abel's leaving right away," he said. "If there's any vaccine at Fort Lauderdale, he'll have it back here by noon tomorrow. And Mr. Evans is going to try to get Captain Dunn to go to Key West."

"Good!" the doctor exclaimed. "I'd like to send you aboard the schooner. You can tell the military down there about the Caloosa. I'll give you a letter to the commandant and some money to pay for the serum."

The *Pilgrim* was ready to sail with the ebb tide that evening. The little Bahamian captain agreed to the professor's request without argument.

"In a part of the world like this," said the Negro skipper with some dignity, "we have to help one another— white people, black people, and Indians. I'll do my best to make a fast trip."

Toby went aboard at sunset. He greeted Gordon, the big Negro mate, and Pedro, the conch seaman, as old friends. They grinned a welcome and put him to work at once, helping them hoist the sails.

They made a southerly reach of it till they cleared Cape Florida and were out in the Gulf Stream. Then, with the trade wind on their quarter, they drove southwest along the keys under full sail. The *Pilgrim* was fast enough. She was logging a steady ten knots as they ran down past Key Largo. Toby was on deck from eight till midnight, sharing the watch with Pedro, who had the wheel.

It was a clear night with a moon. The boy could picture Abel moving up the beach with his long, tireless stride. At the best speed the *Pilgrim* could make, the barefooted mailman would beat her back to Fort Dallas by a day at least. Toby wondered whether

his father, the professor, and Miki-loko would have left
without him before the schooner could return. If Fort
Lauderdale had enough vaccine, that would probably be
the case. The selfish part of him hoped he could still go
with them, but he knew in his heart that lives might be
saved if they made an earlier start.

He turned in at midnight and was wakened again
when the watch changed before dawn. The breeze had
fallen off a bit, but they were still moving steadily west-
southwest under full sail. Captain Dunn was on deck now.

"More wind after sunrise," he told the boy. "We're
making a fast voyage. If all goes well, we should make
Key West by noon."

Toby ate his breakfast and watched the glint of the
first light on the distant keys to starboard. There was a
dark line of trees visible now above the surf and sand—
the Pine Islands. It was only a little after ten when they
sailed into Key West harbor.

Dunn went with Toby to Fort Taylor, leaving the big

mate, Gordon, to take care of the schooner. "Folks down here have light fingers," he explained with a smile. "They'll take anything that isn't watched—even a coil of rope or a bucket."

Fort Taylor had been built some twenty-five years before, to guard this southernmost outpost of the United States. During the war it had been an important base, heavily manned, and there were still a fair number of soldiers quartered there.

It took a few minutes to explain their mission to the sentry at the gate. Then word was relayed inside, and finally a sergeant came to lead them to the commandant's office.

A middle-aged colonel sat behind the desk, his uniform coat unbuttoned in the heat. He frowned as he listened to their story.

"I don't know whether we can help you or not," he said. "Have to get a report from my medical officer. If he's got any fresh vaccine on hand, we might have to go through military channels to release it."

Up to that moment Toby had forgotten the letter in his pocket. He held it out to the colonel and watched a change come over the man's face as he read it.

"Well, now, this is different," he smiled. "Is Dr. Morgan your father? He was with my regiment all through the Battle o' the Wilderness. Saved some of our boys' lives. If he needs medical supplies, I guess we can forget the red tape."

Within an hour Toby and the skipper were on their way back to the schooner. They had their vaccine—a good half of all the fort could provide. And the colonel had refused to take any money for it.

"If I recall my regulations," he grinned, "the Army is to act promptly to aid civilians in times of disaster or emergency. I'll put the facts in my report, and I don't think any of those bookkeepers back in Washington will question that this is an emergency. Give my warmest regards to your father."

They made sail at once. The homeward trip was certain to take longer, for they were forced to tack against the prevailing northeasterly wind. However, the Gulf Stream helped them along now. By sunset, twenty-four hours from the time they had first set out from Fort Dallas, they were nearly abreast of Key Vacas.

All night the *Pilgrim* beat her way up the coast. Sunrise found them off Key Largo, and five hours later, well before noon, they entered Biscayne Bay.

Toby saw a little group of people gathered at the landing when they hove to. His own family was there—Sue and her father—Miki-loko and Abel Harris. As quickly as possible he carried his precious package of serum ashore.

"Were you able to get it?" his father called out eagerly. And his face showed a deep relief at the boy's answer.

"They had no vaccine at Fort Lauderdale," the doctor explained. "Abel had his trip for nothing. But with what you've brought we may still be in time if we start at once."

On the way to the Morgan house Toby had a moment to talk to Miki-loko.

"How do you feel now?" he asked. "Does your arm hurt?"

The young Indian held it out for inspection. "No," he said with firmness. "No hurt."

Toby grinned. He could see that the vaccination looked red and angry, but he knew his friend would die before admitting any pain.

"Well," he laughed, "I'm glad it 'took,' anyhow. You look a heap better than you did a couple o' days ago."

Toby's mother prepared a midday meal for all of them

while they made their plans. Dr. Morgan told them he would go with Miki-loko in the canoe, taking his medicine kit and the vaccine. Toby would be needed to pole the pirogue, which would be carrying supplies for the party. The professor decided he could still take the camera, even though getting pictures was a secondary consideration. Sue and he had both been vaccinated while Toby was away, so none of the group was likely to catch smallpox.

As soon as they had eaten their lunch, they started up the river. By mid-afternoon everything was stowed aboard the boat. The doctor got into the bow of the dugout, Miki-loko took his station in the stern, and the smaller craft shot out into the current with Toby and Evans poling the pirogue in its wake.

"Three o'clock," said the boy. "We ought to get as far as the alligator hammock by dark."

15

Toby's estimate was fairly close. They came out into the lagoon and beached the canoe and the pirogue on the west side of the hammock about an hour after sunset. Miki-loko had a cook-fire started almost as soon as the others were ashore. Sue and her father began preparing supper, but the Caloosa boy beckoned Toby aside.

"No stop here tonight," he urged his white friend. "Miki-loko find trail in dark. We stop here—maybe more Caloosa people get sick."

Toby could understand his impatience, but he was worried about the strain on his own father. Before the meal was ready, he found a chance to talk to him alone.

Dr. Morgan chuckled. "I'm fresh as a daisy," he told the boy. "Miki-loko is right. We ought to push on if he can guide us. Even a few hours at this stage of an epidemic may save some lives. I'm sure Evans will agree if I put it to him squarely."

They talked it over while they ate. The professor was somewhat shocked at the idea of trying to navigate the saw grass channels at night. But Toby pointed out that the Indian boy had done it before.

"Besides," he reminded the older man, "we'll have a good moon most of the time. All that worries me is keeping the canoe in sight."

"Why not mount a light in the stern of the dugout?" Sue put in. "We've got a lantern, you know."

"Good!" said Toby. "And in case the oil doesn't hold out, I'll split some fat pine for torches."

In less than an hour they were in the boats again. Miki-loko threaded his way through the wandering channels with such unerring skill that Professor Evans was constantly amazed.

"It must be more than memory," he commented. "A kind of sixth sense, like the one that guides a homing pigeon. I'm sure very few white men have it, but it seems to be born in an Indian."

"Maybe it's partly instinct," Toby agreed. "But besides that, Miki-loko has wonderful eyesight. He sees everything and remembers what he sees. So every clump of saw grass is a sort of landmark. I think a white man might do it almost as well if he grew up in the wilderness and had to practice seeing and remembering from the time he was old enough to walk."

Ahead of them the lantern glowed faintly, bobbing on the end of a pole that stuck up in the stern of the dugout. By hard work and skillful steering Toby managed to keep within fifty yards—close enough so that they didn't stray into the wrong channel.

After a few hours of it he was pretty tired. He had been on his feet practically since daybreak and had slept only about four hours the night before. His muscles ached, but he made no complaint. This expedition was one that involved life and death, and there was no place in it for thinking of personal comfort.

Midnight came and passed, and still they pushed on. Toby's arms and back felt numb now. His main trouble was to stay awake—to keep his balance and continue the steady rhythm of poling. Once he stumbled and had to catch himself.

"Dad," said Sue quietly, "I think you'd better take that pole now, before Toby falls in the water."

Her father had been napping in the bow of the pirogue. He shook himself awake and hurried aft.

"Sorry, lad," he said. "I'd lost track of time. Should have spelled you before."

The boy was too groggy to protest. He turned over the pole to the older man and slumped down in the bottom of the boat. Within seconds he was asleep.

* * *

It was Sue who shook him awake in the first gray light of dawn. "I think we must be close, now," she said. "I heard Miki-loko give a hail a minute ago, but there wasn't any answer."

Toby stretched to get the stiffness out of his muscles. "Ugh!" he mumbled, wincing. "I feel as if I'd been run over by a train!"

Standing up, he could see the outlines of a big, tree-clad island in the half-darkness ahead. The lantern on the canoe had burned out, but there was a flickering glow close to the water. There must be a fire near the landing place.

The Indian boy shouted again, and this time a high-pitched, tremulous call came back from the shore. It sounded more like a sobbing cry than words. Toby picked up the spare pole and helped the naturalist drive the pirogue forward. The dugout was already at the landing.

Peering ahead through the rising dawn mist, Toby could see only three people there by the water's edge—his father, Miki-loko, and one other. It was an Indian woman, bowed with grief.

They beached the pirogue and got out. Miki-loko had

his arm about the weeping woman. It was his mother, Toby realized. She was telling the boy something in short, muffled sentences, broken by sobs. At last Miki-loko straightened his shoulders and faced the others, his face stark and grim in the flickering firelight.

"Many are dead," he said harshly. "The Chief Mikko, my father, lies sick in his house. The others—all of them —have run away. They hide somewhere in the swamps. Only this woman, my mother, has stayed."

Dr. Morgan had his medicine kit in his hand. He took charge now, a firm authority in his voice.

"There's no time to lose," he said. "Miki-loko, I must vaccinate your mother at once. Tell her it's all right."

The Caloosa boy showed her the scab on his arm and explained the matter in a few words. Then, in docile obedience, she drew back her robe and exposed her shoulder. It took the doctor only half a minute to make the scratch and apply the vaccine.

"Now," he said, "let's go find your father."

The town had a pitiful look in the early morning light. The doors of the *chi-kees*—the thatched huts—gaped black and empty. There were bits of clothing, cooking pots, broken arrows, and other remnants strewn about on the ground, abandoned by the fleeing Indians. Even the dogs were gone.

Miki-loko led the way to the chief's house and hesitated a moment before the deerskin that was draped over the doorway. Then he drew a deep breath, pushed the curtain aside, and went in. The others waited till he reappeared a few seconds later.

"He is alive," the young Caloosa told them. "But he feels the sickness is upon him. Come quickly and give the white man's medicine."

The man lay on a pile of skins in a corner of the dark

house. His big frame looked wasted and thin, and his eyes were lustreless. The doctor knelt beside him, felt his pulse, and laid a hand on his forehead.

"Fever," he announced briefly. "But no spots yet. There's just a chance, if I vaccinate him at once."

Again Miki-loko displayed his arm and said a few words in the Caloosa tongue. The chief nodded heavily, as if he were past caring what was done to him. And immediately Dr. Morgan set to work. When he straightened up, he turned to Miki-loko.

"You must make him believe that he will get well," the doctor said. "Right now he's given up. Have your mother cook some broth and tell him he must eat. I've given him medicine to reduce the fever, and it's still possible he'll live if he can keep up his strength."

Toby translated his father's words, and Miki-loko finally understood. He told the woman what was needed, then went in to talk to the chief. After a few minutes he came out again, his usually impassive face twisted with unhappiness.

"It is as you say," he told the doctor. "He has no hope, but he will try to eat. Come, Toh-bee. The dead must be buried."

They found the bodies of a dozen Indians, braves, squaws, and children, on a hastily erected platform of poles near the edge of the clearing. With the professor's help they carried them on crude stretchers to the ancient burial mound of the Caloosa, a short distance south of the village. There they laid them to rest under clean earth.

The sun was high when they finished, and Evans took a few photographs of the deserted houses. Sue was busy at the cook fire, helping the Indian woman prepare a meal for their party. Miki-loko drew Toby aside.

"My father," he said brokenly, "thinks he will die before the sun is gone. He says I am the new chief of the
Caloosa people and I must make a speech of welcome to
our white friends."

Toby gripped the other lad's arm. "Gosh," he said, "I
know how you feel. But you don't have to do it yet. Let's
wait till evening—see how he is then."

At noon they ate venison stew and coontie bread.
Before he went in to visit his patient again, Dr. Morgan
asked Miki-loko if he could find the hiding places where
the rest of the Indians had gone.

"If you could get them to come back," he said, "we'd
have a chance to vaccinate all of them. As it is, I expect
others will contract the disease and die, off there in the
swamps."

The boy agreed to try and set off immediately in his

canoe. Toby offered to go with him, but Miki-loko was firm in his refusal.

"I must go alone," he said. "If they come, it will be because their chief has sent for them."

He took no weapons, only a strangely carved conch shell that gave a weird, far-carrying sound when he blew into one end.

Toby, still short of sleep after his long night's work, lay down in the shade of a palm and took a nap. It was nearly sundown when he woke to a sound of guttural voices.

At the landing were half a dozen canoes, and striding up into the village was Miki-loko, followed by a huddled, scared-looking group of Indians. He halted them outside the chief's house and stepped softly in.

Toby had hurried to join his father. "Is—is Chief Mikko still alive?" he asked in a whisper.

The doctor nodded. "His fever's lower, and he managed to keep the broth down. It all depends now on his will to live."

Minutes dragged by while they waited. The Indians were ill at ease. Obviously Miki-loko had brought them here against their will. Some stood staring at the ground. Others stole furtive glances about the clearing, acting as if they were ready to bolt at any instant. Toby was uneasy, too, wondering what kept his friend so long inside. He had a feeling that Mikko was dead and that his son was putting on the ceremonial robes that would mark him as chief. When a glow of bright-colored cloth and a glint of metal came from the darkness of the doorway, he was sure of it.

Then, in astonishment, he saw that the stately figure emerging from the house was too tall to be his friend. With a firm step, his gaunt face composed and proud, the

Great Chief of the Caloosa came out to stand before his people.

There was a stirring among the Indians, but they kept silent, their eyes fixed on their leader. He began speaking, his voice deep, the words rolling slowly and impressively. Toby could follow only a little of what he said, but the speech stirred him nevertheless.

What had happened, Mikko told them, was well known to his people. The sickness of many spots was an evil no medicine man of their tribe could cure. Already it had taken many of them. It had laid their chief low. He was about to die. But his son, Miki-loko had traveled far to the village of the white men, who had strong medicine. It entered the body through the arm and fought with the devils that made the small spots.

"Look!" he commanded in a loud voice, and pointed to the red mark on his upper arm. "All of you will have this good medicine. It is Mikko's order."

With that he turned, staggering a little, and steadied himself with a hand on his son's shoulder as he went back to his couch.

Dr. Morgan drew a deep breath. "What a man!" he murmured. "I don't know what he told them, but it worked. I guess I've got a job to do now."

When Miki-loko came out, he immediately lined up the Indians and told them to do as the white doctor commanded. It was growing dark when the last vaccination had been made.

"All right," said Dr. Morgan wearily, "I think we may have stopped the epidemic. Toby, I want you to tell Miki-loko what to do. These people can't just sit around looking at their arms. They've got to cook their supper, clean up their houses, burn the clothing and bedding of those who died. Above all, they must be told not to scratch if their arms begin to itch. While you're doing that, I must go in and take another look at the chief."

Miki-loko's mother had quietly helped the doctor while he was at work. Now he took her with him into Mikko's house. Toby could see, when she came back to the cooking fire, that her face was no longer sad. Indian women, he had learned, were less stoical than the braves. They were allowed to laugh and weep, and their expressions gave some clue to their feelings.

Miki-loko, meanwhile, had organized tasks for the people of the village, and they were carrying out his orders. There was a guest house at one end of the clearing. He supervised the laying of clean skins on its pole floor, raised a couple of feet from the ground, and insisted that the white party spend the night there.

By nine-thirty the Indians were in their *chi-kees* and the town lay quiet in the darkness. Toby and Miki-loko walked silently together down to the landing. Off to the east, above the miles of saw grass, the moon was just rising.

"My people will not forget," the young Indian said in a low voice. "Today your father saved my father and the Caloosa tribe. This is a great thing."

Toby hesitated to tell him that vaccination wasn't infallible—that some of them might still die of smallpox. After all, if they believed in the white man's medicine, that was half the battle. He nodded understandingly and kept his peace.

"Guess I'll sleep here in the boat," he finally told his friend with a yawn. "I don't know how you can keep on your feet, the way you've worked for two days and a night. Don't you ever get tired?"

The stern mask of Miki-loko's face broke into a grin, and he nodded sleepily. Then he was gone, padding silently up the bank on moccasined feet.

148

16

Wrapped in a tarpaulin in the bottom of the pirogue, Toby slept soundly through the night. He didn't hear the hoot of a hunting owl or the small splash of a raccoon looking for frogs in the reed-grown shallows. It was the early sun in his eyes and the sound of activity in the village that finally woke him.

He got up, stretching his arms, and drew a deep breath of the fresh morning air. A whiff of wood smoke came to him from the fires. The squaws were getting breakfast, and several of the men, he was glad to see, were preparing their weapons for a hunt. The whole place had a peaceful, normal look.

Half a dozen little Indian children, naked except for G-strings, came running down the slope, stopped suddenly at the sight of him, and froze like a covey of quail. Their solemn black eyes watched him shyly as he passed, going up to the village.

His father seemed thoughtful at breakfast. "I can't believe it yet," he said. "Yesterday they were all scared to death. I mean that literally. From the chief on down they were sure they were going to die. And I guess they would have. Now they're going on as if nothing had happened. It's just a kind of childlike faith, I expect."

149

"What about Mikko?" Toby asked. "Do you think he's going to be all right?"

Sue laughed. "You should have seen the breakfast Naneechee took in to him," she said. "That's his wife—Miki-loko's mother. A big bowl of stew and two kinds of coontie cakes and some sort of herb tea."

The doctor shook his head. "Not what I'd prescribe," he commented, "but maybe he'd starved long enough. I doubt if he'd had anything to eat for four days. These people are beyond me."

Professor Evans finished his meal and began making immediate preparations to take photographs. He persuaded two of the braves to pose with their bows and spears before they went hunting. Then he got pictures of a squaw grinding coontie root, a group of children in front of one of the *chi-kees,* and close-up portraits that showed the silver ornaments worn by some of the women.

Miki-loko slept till nearly noon. When he appeared, he watched the professor taking pictures with deep interest. He had been shown a few of Evans' photographs while he was in Fort Dallas, but it was still hard for him to believe that a lifeless black box could draw so beautifully. After a while he came to Toby with a suggestion.

"You want hunt?" he asked. "We go in canoe—kill O-kaima, the alligator. Maybe your friend bring box in boat—make pictures?"

Toby was delighted with the idea and so were the professor and Sue. They took the camera back to the pirogue, and in a few minutes Miki-loko came down to his dugout. All he carried was a short, heavy spear, for this hunt was to be in the true Indian fashion.

Because he was better at handling the pirogue than Evans, Toby turned down the Caloosa boy's offer to go with him in the canoe. If they were able to get a photograph of the battle, he didn't want it spoiled by having a white boy in it. But just in case Miki-loko got into difficulties, he had the rifle handy, where he could cover his friend from the larger boat.

They followed the dugout for perhaps half a mile, moving slowly as Miki-loko searched the channel banks. Suddenly he held up a warning hand. Toby, standing high in the pirogue, caught a glimpse of a dark, loglike shape sunning on a mud bank, twenty yards ahead.

Very quietly the Indian boy guided the canoe in among the saw grass roots and got out. His feet sank into the mud at every step, but he moved slowly and with such care that he made no sound.

The professor had a plate in the camera. Toby maneuvered the boat's bow to the left, so that there would be an unobstructed view, and they waited, hardly daring to breathe. A silent step at a time, Miki-loko was nearing his quarry.

He was only ten feet away when the alligator stirred, raising its head. They saw the young Indian's muscles tense. He crouched, then leaped forward. With the spear in his left hand he reached out with his right and caught the big beast's hind leg just above the clawed foot. His momentum carried him on across the alligator's tail, and with a jerk of his right arm he flipped the heavy body over on its back.

Toby had picked up the rifle, but there was no need to use it. With one swift, sure stroke, Miki-loko plunged his stabbing spear into the creature's soft underparts. Then he jumped quickly aside to avoid the mighty thrash of the tail. The stricken beast tried to wriggle into the water, but the spear must have reached a vital spot. After a few convulsive heaves the alligator lay motionless, still on its back.

Miki-loko stood up and faced them with a proud grin.

"Tell him to pose," Evans said. "Not that way, but bent over, with his hand on the spear as if he was just driving it in."

With sign language and a few Indian words, Toby succeeded in getting over the idea. The Caloosa boy did as he was asked, and the professor shot several pictures from different angles and distances.

"The light's perfect!" he gloated. "These ought to be the prize photographs in my whole collection!"

Miki-loko now pointed to the foot-thick tail of the dead brute. "Good meat," he said. "Cut-um off."

Toby helped with the job while the others watched admiringly. At last they severed the tail from the body and held it up. It must have weighed seventy pounds.

There was a feast that night in the Caloosa town. The squaws built a big fire and set a huge iron pot over the coals. Into it went chunks of meat cut from the alligator tail, along with onions, cabbage palm hearts, and various herbs for seasoning. When it was cooked, they all gathered around to help themselves. Even the youngest children stuffed their stomachs till they could hardly walk. Toby had never tried alligator stew before, but he found it rich and tasty. Sue agreed with him. The two older men ate only as much as was necessary to be polite.

That afternoon two more canoeloads of the strayed tribe had come in. They must have heard by some mysterious grapevine signal that all was well once more in the village. Dr. Morgan had promptly vaccinated them, and they took full part in the banquet.

When it was over, the chief rose from his place of honor and stood straight and tall. His face was no longer as shockingly haggard as it had been when Toby and the others first arrived.

He did not speak long, for it was apparent his legs

were still weak from his illness. But his words came from the heart.

It was the hope of the Caloosa people, he said, that the white visitors would stay long in their village. Because of the thankfulness in their hearts they would remember the good medicine man, the father of their brother, Toh-bee, as long as the sun crossed the sky and water flowed in the Glades. There was no fitting gift they could make now, but at a later time, when he had talked with the wise men of the Caloosa, his son would bring a message to the white men's town.

When Mikko had finished, Dr. Morgan rose and replied. He spoke in English but slowly and simply, so that Miki-loko could translate his words. His calling, he said, was to help those who were sick—all men, whether their skins were white or red. He knew the Indians had good medicine, for they had saved his son when bitten by the alligator. But there were some things their medicine could not cure. If they needed him again, he would come. It was good that the Caloosa and the white men should be friends.

*   *   *

They stayed in the village two more days, to be sure there was no further outbreak of smallpox. Toby went hunting with Miki-loko and some of the braves, and they brought back two deer, killed on nearby islands. The second morning the two boys ranged to the westward in Miki-loko's canoe, exploring some of the hammocks on the farther edge of the Glades. Only a few miles beyond the water turned salt, the Caloosa boy explained. That marked the beginning of the mangrove swamps fringing the Gulf.

They swung southward following a channel through

the saw grass. Paddling in the bow, Toby glanced ahead and saw a small island that looked interesting. It seemed to rise high above the water, and it was covered with dark old cypress trees and tangled, hanging vines.

"Let's go over there," he suggested, pointing with his paddle, but Miki-loko kept silent. When he repeated the words, the young Caloosa grunted a curt "No" and steered the dugout into another channel, heading away from the hammock.

"What's the matter?" Toby asked. "Why don't you want to land there?"

Reluctantly Miki-loko answered at last. "Bad place," he said. "Nobody go there. All time bad spirits stay on hammock."

Toby was more intrigued than ever, but he knew better than to argue the matter. Bad spirits were very real to his friend, and most Indian superstitions had a basis in fact. There was something sinister about the island— a danger of some unknown kind. Perhaps it was better for a white boy not to try to find out.

When they returned that afternoon, Dr. Morgan was squatting under a tree with Mikko's wife, Naneechee. The Caloosa woman had gathered a dozen kinds of leaves and was showing the doctor how they were used in medicine. They seemed to be getting along splendidly in sign language, so Toby didn't make any effort to interpret. He knew his father had wanted to learn about these herbs for a long time.

That night was their last in the Caloosa village. They said their farewells early the next morning and set out eastward, with Miki-loko going along to guide them on their first day's journey. When they reached the "alligator hammock" late in the afternoon, he turned back, grinning and waving good-by. Earlier he had made

Toby a promise that he would be coming to Fort Dallas for a visit before too long.

They landed and started their evening campfire. As they sat around the blaze after supper, Toby mentioned the forbidden island.

"It was a funny thing," he said. "Miki-loko wouldn't talk at all at first. Then he just said no—there were bad spirits there. I didn't push him, but I'd sure like to explore it sometime and see what all the mystery's about."

Professor Evans was interested. "There's usually a reason for that kind of a taboo," he said. "It could be one of many things—a murder committed there long ago, or something poisonous that grows on the island. Perhaps they've even forgotten what it was themselves. But the legend of the bad spirits still lives on in their minds."

Toby accepted this theory. He had figured it somewhat the same way himself. One could discount the idea of ghosts or spirits. But whatever the evil influence of the hammock might be, he still wanted to go there some day and see whatever he could discover.

He lay awake thinking about it that night, but only for a short while. Then the healthy weariness of the day's work overcame him, and he slept soundly till daybreak. They rose next morning in ample time to reach Fort Dallas before dark, and their homeward trip was uneventful until just before they reached the mooring place above the rapids.

Toby was poling the pirogue at the time. Ahead, near the trees that marked the higher ground, he saw a puff of smoke. The sound of the shot came to them a moment later, and something white was thrashing at the edge of the water. By the time they approached the entrance to the Miami, the hunter was gone. But the body of an egret, stripped of its back and tail feathers, was floating there in the reeds.

Toby reached out for it and held it up. "Plume hunter," was all he said, but there was bitterness in his voice. He passed it over to Evans, and the professor took it, examining the big, limp body.

"This," he said grimly, "has got to be stopped. In a dozen more years there won't be an egret left in Florida. Perhaps I have no influence in Washington, but my friends at the Smithsonian do. I'll get a letter off by the first mail that goes north."

They unpacked the pirogue at the mooring place and carried their loads down to Fort Dallas. There was considerable interest in their arrival among the people at the store.

"Another day," said Mr. Peacock, "and we'd have sent a search party after you. How'd you find things back yonder?"

They explained why they had stayed so long at the Caloosa village and went on to their houses. Toby helped carry the camera down to the Evans place but got back in time for a late supper. Christian food, served at a table, was a welcome change for his father and himself.

For several weeks there were no more photographic trips. Professor Evans was busy classifying the many pictures he had taken at the Caloosa town and writing up his notes on the habits and living conditions of the primitive Indian tribe.

"Do you know what ethnology is?" he asked Toby with a grin. "It's the science of racial differences and characteristics among humans. I'm really a zoologist myself, but I guess this report on the Caloosa comes under the head of ethnology. By the way, I'm going to need your help on some of the hunting and fishing angles, and we'll sign it together. It won't hurt to have your name known in scientific circles when you go north to college."

Toby was thrilled. He worked with the naturalist for hours, helping get the details accurate. When the report was finished, it filled many neat pages, and with some thirty photographic prints it was bundled up and sent off to Harvard early in December. A week later there was a large manila envelope for Toby in the mail.

He stared at the New York postmark, then opened the envelope with shaking hands. The dignified-looking publication he took out was the quarterly review of a famous scientific society. And tucked away toward the end was his article about the caracara and the otter family. Under the title he read his own name—"Tobias Morgan."

Speechless with pride, he rushed to his father and mother and held out the opened magazine. His parents were as much impressed as he was, and Dr. Morgan read the article aloud, pausing now and then to praise the vivid words in which Toby had described the bird's attack and the mother otter's valiant defense.

"Gee!" said Toby. "Did I write that? It looks and sounds so much better when it's in print!"

He had been too excited to look farther in the envelope, and it was Betsy who discovered there were other enclosures.

"Look!" she cried. "A letter! They hope you'll send them some more things like this. And here's a check! It's for fifteen whole dollars! Toby—you'll be rich!"

17

Eager to share his triumph, Toby hurried down to the Evans' house that evening. When the congratulations were over, the professor talked to him seriously.

"I think you've made a wise choice of a career," he said. "But remember there's a long, hard road ahead of you. A few articles like this won't buy groceries for a family if you have one. In order to make a living in science, you must study for years, get a master's or doctor's degree. You'll probably teach for a while. Then, if there's a specialty in which you've proved you can make a real contribution, you may get the backing of some university or museum to do field work. I just want to be sure you realize what you're getting into."

Toby thought it over for a minute or two. "Thanks," he told the naturalist. "I guess I don't mind hard work, if it's the kind of work I like. After all, my dad had to spend a long time learning to be a doctor—college, medical school, internship, and everything. Besides, I want to learn to write well. Maybe I can piece out my income by doing stories about animals—not just in scientific journals but in popular magazines. I've heard they pay pretty well, and I think people would like to read about nature if the stories were exciting enough and true at the same time."

The professor laughed and patted his shoulder. "You'll make it," he said. "A boy who doesn't get discouraged easily can be just about anything he wants in a free, growing country like ours. So—more power to you!"

It was the middle of December when this talk took place, and Christmas was only ten days away. The two families of Northerners planned to celebrate the holiday together at the Evans' house.

Already Sue and Betsy were whispering in corners, wrapping mysterious parcels, and working on paper chains and other decorations. Toby was determined they should have a tree, and he didn't mean to settle for a palmetto. He spent days exploring the nearby woods, on foot or in the canoe, and finally he found what he was looking for. It was a bushy little pine growing in a sunlit clearing, where it had enough room to fill out without being spindly, like most pine saplings. He marked the spot and returned next morning with an ax.

Caesar accompanied him in the dugout. The big hound enjoyed these trips, even when no hunting was involved. As soon as the canoe touched the bank, he was out with a bound, ranging through the brush with his nose to the ground.

Toby located his tree and felled it with two or three careful strokes of the ax. He thought wistfully of the balsam firs that had been their Christmas trees in other days, of the sharp cold of December mornings, of the snow-covered roads and cheerful sleigh bells. Here the temperature was already in the seventies and would go higher by afternoon. And the tree, with its sparse little clumps of long needles, was a poor substitute for the thick blue-green softness of a balsam. Still, it was an evergreen. Once set up and decorated it would have to do.

He picked it up and was carrying it down to the dugout when he heard Caesar give tongue a couple of hundred yards back in the woods. There was an excited, eager tone in the hound's baying that sounded as if he might be on the track of something big.

Toby dropped the tree by the canoe and hurried toward the sound. He had brought no gun on this trip, but he kept the ax in his hand, in case a weapon should be needed.

When he finally sighted Caesar through the brush, the dog was no longer running. He had paused at the edge of a small stream and was casting back and forth. But he kept on baying. The scent must still be strong in his nostrils.

As soon as Toby came up, he saw something that brought a low whistle to his lips. There in the muck at the margin of the stream was a fresh, clear track—the well-marked footprint of a bear. It was six or seven inches long, and the four claw-holes were so newly made that they hadn't yet filled with water!

Toby grabbed Caesar by the collar and dragged the unwilling dog away. "Come on, boy," he whispered. "We'll go home and get the rifle. No point in scaring him off now."

He left the canoe at the head of the rapids, tied Caesar firmly to a tree, and ran all the way to the house with the little pine bouncing on his shoulder. An hour later he was back with the Winchester.

Black bears, he knew, were common enough in middle Florida, but they rarely came this far south. December was when they usually denned up for the winter. This one, he thought, wasn't a very large bear—possibly a yearling cub. It might have been driven away from its regular feeding grounds by older animals and made its way down the wooded ridges till it reached the Miami country.

When Toby reached the canoe, there was no sign of Caesar. The big dog had chewed through the stout rope and was gone. Probably by now he had chased the bear clear out of Dade County.

In some disgust the boy picked up his paddle and drove the canoe swiftly northward. He landed at the same spot as before. As he ran up through the thickets, he caught the faint, far-off baying of the hound. It was well to the north now, at least half a mile away. There was nothing he could do but follow the sound as fast as possible.

He went at a loping trot, skirting the thickets and sticking to more open country. At first he didn't seem to be gaining. Then he heard the hound's voice change to a series of sharper barks. Caesar must have brought the animal to bay.

Toby hurried his pace and at last, sweaty and panting, he came in sight of a dark limestone ledge half-concealed in the brush. Caesar was jumping about in great excitement. Sure that the bear must have climbed a tree, Toby cocked his rifle and stood staring upward at the branches. Then he realized that the dog's main interest was the ledge.

Stepping cautiously nearer, he saw a gap, perhaps a foot high, at the base of the rock. It was nearly hidden by grass and bushes, but there might be room, he thought, for a small bear to squeeze through.

He came nearer and crouched to peer into the black opening. Caesar, encouraged by his master's presence, chose that moment to make a charge at the cave. He got his head and shoulders inside. Then, with a sudden yelp of dismay, he pitched backward in a half somersault.

Toby was scarcely ten feet from the ledge, kneeling on one knee, when the beast came out. He saw the black head and angry eyes—the teeth bared in a snarl. Then he lifted the rifle.

"Get out o' the way!" he yelled at the dog. But Caesar had recovered enough to be brave again. He sprang growling at the bear's throat and was knocked heels over head by the swipe of a paw. That gave Toby a split-second chance. He fired straight into the animal's open jaws, and at such close range one bullet was enough.

The bear coughed, pitched forward, kicked once or twice, and lay still.

"Yippee!" yelled Toby, giving rein to his pent-up excitement. "Bear meat for Christmas dinner!"

He skinned the animal carefully and found it was larger than he expected. It weighed, he thought, about two hundred pounds—big for a yearling. It was fat and well fed, too, and its coat was glossy black.

"Gee!" the boy exulted. "What a rug that skin will make! Just the thing for Mom to step out o' bed on when we have a nippy morning!"

He had been wondering what he could give his mother for Christmas, and now it seemed his problem was solved. He cut away the good meat in the hams and loins and left the rest for the buzzards. Two trips were required to carry the meat and the hide back to the canoe.

Caesar had been raked by the bear's claws in his first encounter, but the cuts didn't seem to be deep. The dog was in fine spirits when they started for home.

*   *   *

Toby's idea of having roast bear for the Yuletide feast was squelched when he talked to Jack Punch at the landing that evening.

"Lemme tell ye about b'ar meat," said the old-timer. "It ain't fit fer even a hawg to eat till it's been hung a spell. Hang up yer meat in a tree, with good stout nettin'

to keep the flies off it, an' leave it thar till it's ripe. Then cook it in a pot with plenty o' b'ar fat, an' ye've got a right tasty meal."

Regretfully he followed directions. Next day he scraped all the scraps of fat off the inner side of the skin and took it to the Seminole camp, where one of the old Indians of his acquaintance agreed to tan it in the native fashion for a dollar in cash.

The boy still had the problem of providing suitable fare for a real Christmas dinner. It didn't seem fitting to sit down to hog and hominy on such an occasion. That afternoon before sunset he loaded the fowling-piece and set off in the dugout to try to locate a turkey roost.

For two hours he paddled northward along the edge of the pine ridge watching the sky ahead for birds. There were thousands of them—herons, spoonbills, and pelicans—heading for their roosting places in the trees. They filled the air with their croaking and squawking as they quarreled over space on the limbs. But there wasn't a turkey among them.

It was almost too dark to see anything when he turned back. Perhaps it was because turkeys were so much in his mind that his ears picked up a very faint sound that might have been a gobble. He was a mile above the Miami rapids when he heard it, and he sat tense in the canoe, drifting slowly southward and listening as hard as he could. At last it came again, unmistakable this time. Somewhere close at hand in the dark pines there were turkeys settling down for the night.

Quietly Toby dipped his paddle again and went on. By the time he hauled out the canoe, his plan was made. He would come back before dawn and try to shoot one when they began stirring at daybreak.

There was no alarm clock in the Morgan household,

so the boy slept very little that night. He woke a dozen times to look out at the stars. Finally, about four o'clock, he got out of bed and dressed in silence. When he left the house with his gun, Caesar tried to follow him, but he shut the hound up in the kitchen. It was still dark as he got into the dugout and paddled up the shore.

Everything depended on silence now. He pulled in to the bank a hundred yards below the spot where he had heard the gobbling, tied the canoe to a root, and moved noiselessly into the woods. A gray tinge was coming into the sky, enabling him to see where he was going. Careful not to step on a stick or rustle the brush, he approached the place.

He had no way to tell how far in from the water the roost might be. There was only his memory of the sound, and when he paused to search the trees ahead, he began to think he had miscalculated. Bushy tufts of pine needles partly obscured his view of the branches. He shifted his position a yard or two to the right, and even though he thought he had made no sound, something moved on a tree limb a hundred feet away.

Toby cocked the gun and took aim, all in one motion. It was none too soon, for the turkeys—four or five of them—were already spreading their wings when he pulled the trigger. By luck he hit the biggest one. It tumbled to the ground while the others sped away like bullets.

The boy rushed forward and reached the crippled bird almost as soon as it landed. Instantly he seized it by the leg, for he knew a wounded turkey that scuttled into the brush was almost impossible to find. But it fluttered its huge wings only once before it died.

Grinning with pride, he carried the twenty-five-pound tom back to the canoe. The first daylight glinted on its bronze breast feathers. He thought then, as many had thought before him, that the wild turkey was the noblest of all American birds.

*   *   *

Two days later the big bird, stuffed and roasted to a crackling golden brown, graced the long table in the Evans' dining room. Christmas morning had dawned clear and balmy. A soft trade wind rustled the palm fronds, and great red hibiscus flowers made the dooryard a riot of color. The gifts had already been distributed.

Toby had done the best he could. The bearskin rug was his present to his parents, and he had hewed out a small log to make a doll's cradle for Betsy. He knew how Sue liked to fish, and he dipped into his hard-earned savings to buy her a rod and tackle at the store.

His own gifts took his breath away. His father gave him a new double-barreled shotgun to replace the one he had presented to Miki-loko. His mother and Besty had knitted socks for him. Professor Evans smiled at the boy's pleasure in the fine zoology textbook he gave him. The last present he opened was a soft deerskin hunting shirt sewn by Sue's own hands.

After dinner they gathered around the little parlor organ brought by Mrs. Evans from the North. While she played, they joined in singing Christmas carols, and in a corner the bright paper decorations shone in the brave light of candles on Toby's little pine tree.

Later Toby and Sue made it a real Florida Christmas by trying out the new rod on Biscayne Bay and winding up with a swim in the warm surf of the beach.

"It's funny," said the girl as they trudged homeward with a good catch of snappers. "I thought I'd be homesick today. But I didn't miss the cold and snow a bit. Last year I went skating on the lake at home. This year it was a dip in the Gulf Stream—and still it's seemed like Christmas!"

Toby nodded. "I guess it isn't where you are or what the temperature is that counts," he said. "It's being with people you love and giving them things. Last year we were here, but we'd hardly got settled and still felt like strangers. Dad was pretty sick then, too, and Christmas fell sort of flat. Maybe it was the carols that did it today. They made me remember whose birthday this is."

18

Even in South Florida, midwinter sometimes brings chilly days. In the weeks that followed Christmas and the New Year, there were frosts as far down the peninsula as Lake Okeechobee. Farmers who drove their oxcarts into Fort Dallas told of ruined orange groves a hundred miles to the north, and even on the shores of Biscayne Bay the settlers huddled around open fires. Then the cold snap passed, almost as quickly as it had come.

Toby watched the sun climb a little higher up the sky at noon each day. He was eager for spring to come, and with it the migrating birds that meant so much to Professor Evans.

The short winter season had been dry, and now, at the beginning of February, fires spread for miles through the Everglades. They could see gray clouds of smoke that covered the sky to the northward. The dead saw grass burned like tinder. Nobody knew how the fires started—lightning perhaps, or careless plume hunters, might be to blame. But they were a yearly sign that spring was close at hand.

The first real evidence of the changing season was a soft mist of green on the branches of the cypresses. Then one morning a flight of white-breasted tree swallows came darting and whirling over the Glades, headed north. They were the first of all the migratory birds to appear, and Toby hurried to the Evans' house to report their presence.

The naturalist had spent weeks preparing for this day. The camera and plate-box were quickly carried to the pirogue, and with Toby wielding the pole and Sue holding the binoculars ready, they moved out into the channels among the saw grass.

The swallows were there in huge clouds, but they flew so high and so fast that a photograph was impossible. Evans had to content himself with observing them through the powerful glasses and writing a detailed report in his notebook.

"They're feeding on insects up there," he announced. "Probably they don't come up across the Gulf until the first flies hatch out to give them food for the journey."

From that time on, Toby, who had seen it all happen the previous spring, could foretell almost from day to day what new visitors from the south would be flying in. They came in regular order—the pintails first, followed by the sandpipers and curlews—then the robins and bluebirds and red-winged blackbirds.

Occasionally the professor was able to get a decent picture. He caught a flock of pintail ducks feeding in the water of a lagoon, and once they had a real piece of luck, even though the subject was not a true migrant. Poling quietly among the reeds, they were startled by a deep-voiced ringing *c-r-r-ruck* that came from a few yards away.

Evans turned quickly to the camera and motioned to Sue to have a plate ready. As Toby edged the boat around a clump of saw grass, a gigantic bird came into view. It was a sand-hill crane, fully four feet tall, standing on long, jet-black legs in the shallow water. All its plumage was a silvery gray except for a bright red patch above the eye. So intent was the huge bird on its frog-fishing that Evans had time for a perfect exposure.

It was one of the few really notable photographs he got during those weeks, but he seemed far from disappointed. Like Sue and Toby he was happy enough just to watch the surging tide of life and color that swept over the Glades with the advance of spring.

The boy was too busy guiding the pirogue to jot down any notes while they were on the water. But he was careful to remember everything he saw. Each evening he wrote a record of his observations, setting down the date, the time of day, the weather, and the exact location for every new bird they sighted. Then he described its coloring, size, voice, flight characteristics, and feeding habits as accurately as possible.

It was a lot of work but he enjoyed it. He knew that this was good training for the career he so earnestly hoped to follow.

When the warbler migration began, they were busier than ever. The pirogue was abandoned now, for the little songbirds flocked in the palms and pines and orange trees along the coastal ridge. They came in waves, sometimes four or five species in a single day. It took a quick and accurate eye to spot the difference between a yellow palm warbler and a Kentucky warbler, for example. Both had yellow breasts, though the Kentucky was more sharply marked. And the Canada warbler was hard to distinguish from either of them.

Professor Evans wound up with thirty-seven different warblers on his list. Toby and Sue, who worked together, were handicapped by a less efficient pair of field glasses, but they were close behind the naturalist with a total of thirty-three.

By the middle of March the sun was almost overhead at noon, and its blazing midday heat was more than the older people could stand. While they took their siestas in the shade, Sue and Toby continued to fish and swim, their skins already burned brown. Sue's mother insisted on her wearing a wide hat of panama straw when she went outdoors, but the girl hung it on a limb as soon as she was out of sight of the house. Her mop of dark curls protected her from sunstroke. And to Toby's eye, at least, her deep tan was wonderfully becoming.

Already the Evans family was beginning to talk of going home to Boston. Toby hated to think about it, and by mutual consent he and Sue never discussed the matter.

Sometimes they went back into the Glades in Toby's canoe, for though the spring migration was past, they could never resist the thrill of the teeming life that went on there under the vast sky.

They were drifting in a narrow channel through the saw grass one afternoon, watching the antics of a pair of dark, curve-billed glossy ibis, when another dugout thrust out from a bend ahead and nearly ran into them. Toby gave a shout of joy, for the lone paddler was Mikiloko.

The Indian boy had grown and put on muscle in the last few months. He was a full-fledged warrior now and dressed as befitted a chief's son. In answer to their questions he told them that all was well in the Caloosa village. His father had completely recovered, and the magic medicine of the white doctor had stopped the sickness before it could spread among others in the tribe. He had come, he said, to visit his friends and to bring a message from Mikko, his father.

In company the two canoes returned to the Miami and the settlement. As a gift the young Caloosa had brought two turkeys and a tasty piece of alligator tail. Mrs. Morgan shuddered privately at the thought of eating it. But when Toby had cooked the delicacy in an iron pot over an outdoor fire, she tried a mouthful and found it better than she expected.

After supper Miki-loko rose with full Indian ceremony and delivered his father's message. It was a special invitation to the doctor, Professor Evans, Toby, and Sue to come back with the boy to the Caloosa town. The serious tone in which he said the words made it sound like a royal command. And even though the naturalist was busy with preparations for his return to the North, he agreed to make the journey.

*   *   *

They launched the pirogue at dawn of the second day after Miki-loko's arrival. It was a clear, cool morning, vibrant with color and sound. The brilliant red tongues of the air plants hanging from trees on the riverbank were backed by the new green of cypress leaves. And from all across the Glades came a cheerful singing of birds, a croaking of frogs, and the harsh cries of herons.

Miki-loko led the way and Toby followed, poling the boat with long, steady strokes that ate up the miles. They stopped before noon for lunch at the familiar hammock where the white boy and the Indian had first met. When they went on, Sue asked to ride in the dugout, and Miki-loko was proud to have her as a passenger.

That afternoon they saw numbers of alligators along the muddy banks, but the Indian lad said there was plenty of food at the village, so they made no stops for hunting. Once, when Miki-loko called to them and pointed, Toby saw a young buck in the water, swimming between islands. It was too far away for a shot. Suddenly its antlered head went up, it gave a faint bleat of pain and terror and disappeared, leaving only a ring of ripples on the surface. O-kaima, the alligator, had made another kill.

The day passed without further incidents, and as evening approached they could make out the dark mass of trees on the Caloosa Island far off against the glow of sunset. Darkness came before they reached it, but their coming was expected. A pair of fat pine torches flared by the landing, and a crowd of half a hundred Indians stood there waiting to welcome them.

When the ceremonial greetings were over, the white party was led to the guest house. It was a new *chi-kee,* built since their last visit. It looked nearly as large as the chief's house, and inside there were two rooms, divided by deerskins hung from the roof poles.

Miki-loko pointed out this arrangement solemnly but with obvious pride. It must have been his own idea that the white girl should have the privacy of a separate sleeping place.

In the cleared central area of the village all was bustle as the squaws worked by torchlight to prepare a feast. Luckily the visitors all had good appetites, for there were mountains of food of every kind. Toby, dipping his hands in the great stew kettle, found pieces of venison, alligator tail, and what he thought was 'possum. At least he hoped so. There seemed to be fewer dogs than usual around the village, but he put that idea out of his mind and ate with relish.

On a separate pile of hot stones there were roast turkeys and ducks. And nearby the diners found cabbage palm hearts, coontie cakes, and green coconuts opened and ready to eat.

When the whole population was gorged with food, Chief Mikko rose and faced them. Instantly the chattering ceased, and even the children turned respectfully toward their leader.

With the firelight shining on his copper features and the barbaric finery that decked his massive frame, the chief was an impressive figure. He looked, Toby thought, as strong and kingly as before his sickness.

The speech he made was brief. Again he expressed the pleasure of the Caloosa people in having their white friends among them. At the return of the sun they were to enjoy themselves in any way they liked, with games, hunting, and fishing, or making pictures with the black box. But, he added, when the sun reached the top of the sky there would be a council at which the guests and all the elders and braves of the tribe were to be present. Then he wished them pleasant sleeping and turned to enter his house.

Toby didn't go to sleep at once. He was comfortable enough on his skin bed in the corner of the guest house, but he lay there wondering about the council to be held the next day. Something big and important must be in the wind, for he knew the Indians never took such a gathering lightly. From what he had heard, councils were held only when some grave decision must be reached—peace or war or the appointment of a new chief.

Surely no danger threatened the tribe now, and Mikko could hardly be thinking of retiring.

Finally the boy gave up the puzzle and dropped into slumber. It was growing light when he woke. The village dogs were yapping, and he could hear the voices of children at play. He got up, stretched, and went down to the landing to wash. There he found Miki-loko putting a big fish net into his canoe.

"Come," said the young Indian with a grin. "I show you how to catch many fish—Caloosa way."

There was no mention of breakfast, and after the tremendous meal he had eaten the night before, Toby was far from hungry. He helped push the dugout off and got in, taking the bow paddle. A short time later Miki-loko

steered into a narrow, twisting channel that led westward toward the distant mangrove islands. And when
they had gone two or three miles, he pulled in to the
shore.

At this point, Toby saw, the watercourse they had
been following was only about fifteen feet wide, and the
current ran deep and fast between high banks. The
young Indian was tying one end of the net to a mangrove
root. It must have been used for the same purpose before, for Toby could see worn places in the bark. Miki-
loko attached a stone to the lower corner of the net and
dropped it in the swift-flowing water. Then he shot the
canoe quickly across to the opposite bank, paying out the
net as he did so. Again he weighted the lower corner and
took the upper edge of the net in one hand, holding on
to a root with the other.

Toby had swung around in the bottom of the dugout
so that he could watch. They sat there in silence for close
to a minute. Then he saw the Indian boy's muscles twitch
as the grass rope tightened in his grip. Quickly he
hauled the canoe across, pulling in the net hand over
hand, and when he reached the middle, a big fish came
struggling out of the water. Its head and gills were fast
in the meshes.

The fish was a twenty-pound tarpon that made Toby's
eyes pop. He killed it with a blow of his hunting knife
and pulled it free. At once Miki-loko paddled back, setting the net again.

That particular channel must have been a sort of high-
way for fish coming upstream from the Gulf. In half an
hour they pulled in more than a hundred pounds—
twenty or thirty fish of half a dozen kinds. It seemed a
shame to Toby. He preferred to give them a sporting
chance with rod and reel, and he knew the big tarpon

would have given him a terrific fight. But Miki-loko, who fished only for food, was satisfied.

With the canoe practically full of gleaming beauties, they stowed the net and paddled back against the current. Once they were out of the channel, Toby rested a moment and looked up at the sun. It must be nearing eleven o'clock, he thought.

"Got to get back soon or we'll be late for the council," he remarked. "What's it all about, Miki-loko?"

There was no answer from the paddler in the stern. When Toby looked over his shoulder, he saw that his friend was watching the water ahead, refusing to meet his glance. His mouth was tightly closed, and his face looked as if it had been carved from wood.

Whatever was to happen at the Caloosa council, he wouldn't find it out from the son of the chief.

19

At the landing they handed over their big catch of fish to the squaws to clean. Miki-loko walked with Toby as far as the guest house, then glanced at the high sun and hurried off to his own quarters to dress for the council.

Sue had prepared a snack for her father and the doctor, and they were eating it when the boy entered.

"Hey," he said, "save some for me. I went off without any breakfast."

"We were looking all over for you," Sue pouted. "You could have helped us pose some of these wild youngsters. Besides, if you were going fishing, I think you might have invited me."

"Only room for two in the canoe," he replied, his mouth full of bacon and corn pone. "Sure hauled in a mess o' fish, though. One of 'em was a tarpon that big!"

No doubt the girl had a tart answer ready, but at that moment they heard the hollow booming of a drum. The sound seemed to roll around them like soft thunder. After the space of a breath it came again and then again, repeated at regular intervals. Looking out, the boy saw a brave squatting by a big hollow log at the other end of the clearing. A skin was stretched taut over the end of the log, and when the man struck it with the flat of his hand, the deep roar shook the leaves on the trees.

From all the houses warriors were now striding out in their finest array. Their skins glistened with grease, and there were silver bands around their naked arms. Some had robes of otter or panther skin draped over their shoulders. Eagle and egret feathers adorned their hair. Most startling of all were the streaks of white and yellow clay painted on their faces.

"What a picture!" exclaimed Professor Evans. "I've simply got to take it! Sue, help me get the camera ready."

Toby saw Miki-loko coming toward their door. His apparel was even more striking than that of the other braves. The great feather headdress he wore glowed with many colors, and a heavy silver chain was looped around his neck, hanging down on his bare chest. He was the son of a chief and he looked the part.

"The council of the Caloosa is ready," he told them gravely. "The white doctor and you, Toh-bee, will come now. Your friend, too, if he wishes, but women cannot sit in the council circle."

Sue nodded. "I'd expected that," she whispered to Toby. "Here's my comb. Fix your hair and tuck in your shirt."

He grinned, conscious for the first time of his own sloppy appearance. Hastily he did his best to make himself tidy. Then he was following his father toward the gathering of warriors.

The great drum boomed on, its tempo quickening now. Miki-loko showed the Morgans where to sit, and they squatted cross-legged, facing the center of the broad circle. Finally, when all were in place, the chief made his appearance. Most of them were shaded by the trees that overhung the clearing, but Mikko moved forward to stand resplendent in the blazing sun. The magnificence of the tall figure made Toby catch his breath.

Slowly the chief raised his arm, and the drum was silent. With the look of an eagle on his proud face, Mikko let his glance move deliberately around the circle. They sat as if hypnotized, without a sound or a movement.

His voice was low and resonant as he began to speak. The words were delivered so slowly that Toby was able to whisper a crude translation to his father as the talk went on.

"We are the last of the Caloosa," said the chief. "Here our people have lived for more seasons than there are leaves on a pine tree. We have heard from our grandfathers who were told by their grandfathers of things long past. We have heard how our people hunted the great beasts—beasts larger than houses, with teeth longer than a tall man, curved like the new moon. The bones of their legs were big as the trunks of trees, and they walked in deep water without fear of the alligator."

"Sounds like elephants!" Toby murmured in his father's ear.

"Or mammoths," Dr. Morgan breathed. "Their bones have been found in Florida. But a hundred thousand years ago? It's impossible!"

"Many seasons passed," Mikko went on, "and the Caloosa grew strong. We were the strongest of all the tribes from the big water of Okeechobee to the end of the land. Then the white men came in their great canoes. They wore shirts of iron and carried both guns and spears. But in the swamps they could not fight against the Caloosa. Many times they tried, and many were left dead. Then they went away.

"Now we know that not all the white men are bad. We know that we can live at peace with them and that they will leave us to our hunting and fishing."

He paused and looked toward Toby's father.

"Today," he said, "we are few. One village, only, remains of the Caloosa tribe. But even these few of us would not be here today if the sickness of many spots had not been stopped. For our lives we can thank one man. He came to us four moons ago, not for presents, not because of any debt he owed us. He came because there was goodness in his heart.

"I, Mikko, Chief of the Caloosa, have talked with our wise men. Now I have called you into council so that we may make a gift to the white medicine man who saved us from death. What we give has been guarded by the Caloosa, our fathers and our grandfathers, for more seasons than we can count. But we cannot eat it. We cannot make clothes from it to keep us warm, or houses to shelter us from the rain. It came from white men who were our enemies. To white men who are our friends we shall return it. I, Mikko, your chief, have spoken."

He turned majestically and sat down in the place reserved for him. Toby could feel beads of sweat breaking out on his forehead. A mounting excitement made his pulse beat faster as he sat and waited.

One by one the elders of the tribe rose to speak. In a few words each of them voiced agreement with the chief's decision. When the last one had been heard, Miki-loko got up.

"We will go in five canoes," the chief's son ordered. He indicated the older warriors who were to make up the party, beckoned to Toby and his father, and led the way to the landing.

Professor Evans had chosen not to sit in the council circle. Instead, he had been quietly photographing the proceedings while Sue stood by to hand him plates. Since he had understood nothing of what was said, he looked surprised when the procession moved toward the canoes. Toby stepped closer to Miki-loko.

"Can't they come, too?" he asked.

The Indian boy hesitated, then finally nodded. "But not the black box," he said. "This is a secret place of the Caloosa. If pictures were made, it would not be secret."

The chief and his son occupied the first canoe. Then came Toby and Dr. Morgan, and the others paddled behind them in line. They swung into a channel that led toward the south. Far off on the horizon Toby caught a glimpse of a high, wooded hammock. He was not too surprised when he recognized the place, but again his heartbeat quickened. They were heading for the forbidden island—the one Miki-loko had told him was guarded by evil spirits.

It took longer than he expected to reach it, for they had to thread a twisting maze of creeks. At last the dark, still cypresses loomed close above them. The shore was lined by what looked like an impenetrable jungle of mangroves and trailing vines, but when Miki-loko reached the bank, Toby was amazed to see him push aside a mat of green leaves and disclose a narrow, open path.

When they landed, Toby let his father go ahead while he waited for Sue. He took her hand.

"Got to take care of you," he said. "There are bad spirits here, and I'll bet you're the first female that ever came to this island."

The path, wide enough for only one person at a time, zigzagged through dense mangroves, then went up a slope to the top of a bluff crowned with huge old trees. The shadows were like twilight there between the trunks. Sue's fingers clutched Toby's tighter, and he felt her shiver. No birds called. Except for their muffled footsteps the place was silent as a tomb.

After thirty or forty paces Chief Mikko halted before

a low, roughly built pyramid of coral rocks. He waited till all the party had come up, then motioned to his son. Together they lifted away one stone slab, then another and another. When the last one was removed, Toby found himself staring into a dark opening that was like the mouth of a cave.

For a moment the Indians stood like statues. Then, at a sign from his father, Miki-loko descended into the opening. It must have been four or five feet deep, for only his head and shoulders could be seen. Stooping, he lifted out a small bag of buckskin, so heavy that the muscles stood in ridges on his arms. Three more of the leather sacks followed. Finally the young Caloosa brought up a very old copper box, crusted and corroded almost beyond recognition.

When he had climbed out of the hole, he picked up each of the articles and laid them in a row at the feet of Dr. Morgan. As he did so, the ancient hinge of the box fell away. The lid tipped a little to one side, and they saw a gleam of jewels—red, green, and fiery white.

Toby's breath caught in a gasp. He had no idea of the value of the gems, but if the sacks were full of gold, as he had guessed, he was looking at an enormous treasure.

The chief faced them proudly and stretched out his huge arm. "This is the gift of the Caloosa people to the white doctor," he said simply.

Toby's father stared at the treasure, his face troubled. "I must answer," he told the boy. "Translate for me, son."

Slowly he looked around him at the wise, wrinkled faces of the warriors. "Truly," he said, "this is a great gift. The Caloosa have done well to guard it, for if greedy white men had known it was here, there would have been much fighting and killing. Yet in the hands

182

of good men this gift can be used for curing sickness and for making many people happy.

"It is far more than I deserve, for anything I did to help the Caloosa was my duty as a doctor. But I will accept the gift in the spirit in which it is given. As long as I live, I shall be the friend of Mikko the chief and of all his people."

Toby's voice trembled as he said the words, trying to put into them all the sincerity with which his father had spoken. He must have succeeded, for when he finished the chief and the elders of the tribe nodded as if they were pleased.

"Now," said Mikko soberly, "we will show you what no white man has seen before. I have spoken of the great beasts of long ago. Perhaps you have not believed my words. Look, then."

Slowly the doctor, the professor, Sue, and Toby moved forward. It was so dark in the cavern under the stone pile that they had to stand almost over it before they could see anything. For a moment all four of them stared into the hole. Then Evans broke the silence with a sudden exclamation.

"A tusk!" he cried. "And a thigh bone! Look at them —the biggest I've ever seen!"

Peering into the opening, Toby saw two pale masses. One was an enormous curving thing as thick as his leg and nine or ten feet long. The other, as the chief had said, looked like a whitened tree stump.

"An American mammoth," Evans mused. His voice was low and almost reverent. "*Archidiskodon* would be the scientific name. Pleistocene period. But that was long before we have any record of man on earth."

He turned to Toby. "I suppose there's no chance that they'd let us take these bones away with us," he said wistfully.

The boy shook his head. "Not now," he murmured. "But some day, when they've really learned to trust us, I think we can come back. Maybe we can get photographs of them then. Anyhow I'll keep working on Miki-loko."

20

With solemn care the slabs of coral were replaced over the opening in the cairn. Then at Mikko's command they started back to the canoes.

Toby picked up one of the buckskin bags and found it amazingly heavy. Miki-loko and two of the older Indians carried the others, and Professor Evans took charge of the old copper casket that held the jewels.

When their loads had been placed in the dugouts, they had to rest a moment to catch their breath.

"Gee, Dad," Toby panted, "you and I had better sit mighty steady in the canoe! I'd sure hate to see that sack go to the bottom."

His father smiled. "Just think of it as so much ballast," he answered, "and don't let sudden wealth make you nervous. After all we don't know what's in the bags. Until we do we may as well guess they're full of lead musket-balls.

The boy's jaw dropped. "Golly," he groaned. "Suppose you were right. What an awful comedown that would be!"

The trip back to the village was made safely, and they transferred the treasure to the pirogue. Since it was then well along in the afternoon, Dr. Morgan decided they should spend one more night in the Caloosa town and make an early start next morning.

There was another feast after sunset. Then the big drum began to boom again, and a dozen young warriors, led by the chief's son, bounded out on the hard-trampled earth and performed a war dance for their guests. For more than an hour they crouched, leaped, gestured, and yelled while the rhythm of the drumbeat quickened to a frenzy. At last, streaming with sweat and close to exhaustion, the dancers flung themselves on the ground to rest.

Sue had been sitting beside Toby. As they finished, she gave a long, trembling sigh. "What a day this has been!" she murmured, and the boy agreed with all his heart.

*　　*　　*

Toby slept aboard the pirogue that night. He trusted the Indians completely, but he still felt safer staying close to the treasure. It was always possible that some wandering plume hunter or other white man might pay a visit to the island.

He woke in the first gray light of dawn and saw that some of the squaws were already astir, preparing breakfast. As he started to go ashore, he stumbled over one of the heavy buckskin bags. Sorely tempted, he made a move to untie the thong, then drew back his hand. The gift of the Caloosa had been made to his father, and the privilege of opening it should be his.

By the time Toby had washed, the rest of the visiting party had appeared. They ate breakfast and half an hour later were ready to push off in the boat. All the village, from Chief Mikko down to the youngest toddler, came to the landing to see them off. For the first mile or two Miki-loko paddled in their company, and before he turned back he promised that he would soon come to Fort Dallas for another visit. He waved once as he dis-

appeared around a bend. Then they were alone, poling through the saw grass toward the rising sun.

Toby kept silent as long as he could, wondering when his curiosity would be satisfied.

"Dad," he burst out at last, "aren't you ever going to take a look at those bullets?"

"Bullets!" cried Sue, astonished. "You mean that's all that's in those bags? They were so heavy—well—I thought—"

The doctor chuckled. "I was just waiting to see how soon you'd mention 'em," he said. "Here goes, then. Like opening Christmas presents, isn't it?"

He squatted beside the nearest sack and worked at the knotted thong. Toby let the boat drift while he stood above him. At last the throat of the sack opened, and Dr. Morgan thrust in his hand. It came up filled with broad coins that gleamed yellow in the sunlight.

The professor took one and examined it closely. "Beautiful!" he exclaimed. "Pure Inca gold, minted in Spain in the reign of Charles the Fifth. They must have been captured by the Caloosa sometime around sixteen hundred—maybe earlier."

"How much do you suppose the four bags would be worth?" asked Toby.

"Well, if they weigh fifty pounds apiece, I'd guess $80,000. But they may be heavier, and I'm not sure what gold is worth an ounce right now. Let's just say it's a lot of money."

"And the rubies and diamonds and emeralds!" cried Sue. "They're worth even more, aren't they? Doctor, you're really rich!"

He smiled and shook his head. "I've been as rich as I wanted," he said, "since I got my health back. Besides, you know what I want to do with it. Medicines—surgical equipment—perhaps even a little hospital! Fort Dallas is bound to grow when more people from the North find out about our climate. They'll need medical care."

Toby had gone back to his poling. Now his father looked around at him with a grin. "Maybe there'll be a few dollars left over," he said. "Enough to help you through college."

The boy let out a cheer that was echoed by Professor Evans.

"So science will gain both ways!" the naturalist said. "I foresee a real future for your son. And what a start he'll have with the discovery of those mammoth bones!"

That was a subject Toby had been eager to discuss.

"I've got a lot to learn about prehistoric animals," he said. "When was the Pleistocene period, anyway?"

"It started," Evans answered, "about a million years ago. And it extended up to what geologists call 'recent times'—say fifty thousand years ago, after the last ice age."

"Then," said Toby, "what about the mammoths?"

"That's what stumps me. You know the chief gave a pretty good description of them in that speech he made. And yet it seems utterly impossible that they were living and being hunted here within even the oldest human memory. What happened to the mammoths was something like this. When the glacial cap moved down over northern Europe and Asia, the woolly mammoths in those parts began to die off. Some of them were frozen into the ice and stayed there, pretty well preserved by the cold, until they were discovered by modern scientists. I believe one or two stone arrowheads were found in their carcasses. That makes it look as if early stone-age men did hunt them.

"Long before that, though, some mammoths had crossed over from Siberia to Alaska and gradually spread southward. They developed into the biggest of all the species, the Imperial Mammoth. In the last glacial age most of them disappeared, like their woolly cousins in Asia. But—and I'm just guessing now—a few mammoths wandered down to Florida ahead of the ice. It never reached this far south, so here in the Glades the big animals may have lasted a few thousand years longer."

"Well, then," Toby put in, "why couldn't the ancestors of the Caloosa have hunted them?"

The professor shook his head. "The trouble is," he said, "there's no record of human inhabitants in this part of the world until a great many centuries later. Even then, they probably weren't the same race as the Indians we know.

"About the only way I can explain the chief's story is that the earliest Caloosa found a skeleton buried in the peat of the Everglades. There was enough of it to show it belonged to a gigantic beast, and the tusks must still have been attached to the skull, so they recognized them as teeth.

"Some of the bones, I expect, were carefully kept as tribal relics like those we saw. Then gradually a legend grew up around them, as the story of the discovery was handed down from generation to generation. The old folks probably added artistic touches to the yarn in telling it. I'm pretty sure Mikko really believes that his remote forefathers hunted and killed the mammoth."

Toby continued poling, his face thoughtful. "That's about the way I'd figured it, too," he said. "As soon as I get home, I want to write the whole thing down—exactly what Mikko told us and all I can remember about the tusk and the bone and the rock pile, while it's still fresh. Sure wish we had photographs, though, so we could prove it. Maybe I can write the thing so people will know it's the truth. Do you think any of the universities or scientific societies would be interested?"

The professor laughed. "Would they, indeed! They'll be stirred to their ivy-covered foundations! I wouldn't be surprised if you're kept busy for a while guiding expeditions."

They reached the alligator hammock in time for a hasty lunch at noon, then pushed on. It was growing dark when they tied up to the bank above Fort Dallas.

"I'll stay here and take care o' the gold," said Toby, "if you can carry the camera and plate-box and the jewels. You might stop by Abel Harris's house, Sue, an' ask him to come up an' help me."

The husky mailman got there an hour later and greeted Toby with a grin. "Hear ye got somethin' heavy to tote," he said. "What is it now—rocks?"

"No. Just these little bags. Think you could carry three of 'em?"

The big fellow started to lift one casually and whistled. "Holy cow!" he said. "Sho' are heavy. But I can tote three—with a yoke, that is. Got an ax?"

Within ten minutes he had trimmed and smoothed a bent tree limb so that it fitted over his shoulders. With a coil of rope that was in the pirogue he fastened a bag securely to each end. Then he gripped a third one in his fist, crouched till his neck was under the middle of the yoke and straightened up.

"Come on," he grunted. "Let's go."

With the fourth sack in one hand and his rifle in the other, Toby staggered after him. It was ten o'clock when they finally eased their burdens down in the living room of the Morgan house.

*   *   *

The time was drawing near for the Evans' departure, and Toby was sad to see them go. For one thing he would miss the naturalist's help and encouragement. He had written an account of the fossil discovery with pains-taking care, sticking to facts and trying not to theorize. Then he had drawn neat pictures of the tusk and the thigh bone, giving their approximate size. The professor wanted to take the article north with him and show it to other scientists he knew.

What the boy would miss even more, however, was Sue's companionship. They had shared so many experiences that he felt closer to her than a brother.

The last evening came, and the two families were together at the doctor's house. The *Pilgrim* lay moored off the landing. All the trunks and boxes had been carried aboard, and the schooner would sail with the morning tide.

"Some day," said Sue, "I'm going to come back and live in Florida."

"I sure hope you will," Toby told her. "But I'll see you before that. I'm coming north to college—maybe next fall, if Dad thinks I'm ready."

"That's right," Dr. Morgan put in. "And it's quite likely I'll make the trip with you. Now that the state has given me title to the Caloosa treasure, I want to buy hospital supplies. Philadelphia is the place for that, but there's no reason we shouldn't get up to Cambridge for a day or two."

"Dad—" Toby began. Then he reddened and hesitated. "I know you've expected me to go to your old college—the University of Pennsylvania. I've always thought I'd like Penn, too, but—well—"

His father's eyes twinkled. "It's perfectly all right, son," he said. "Harvard is a great university, and I can see it holds certain attractions for you."

He looked at Sue, and it was her turn to blush. "If Toby *didn't* come to Harvard," she said with spirit, "I think I'd move to Philadelphia!"

www.ingramcontent.com/pod-product-compliance
Lightning Source LLC
Chambersburg PA
CBHW060559190726
48283CB00003B/1082